'You clearly have no idea how much old-fashioned Victorian nightgowns on young, sexy blue-eyed redheads turn me on.'

His expression was no longer humorous, but quietly, deadly serious, and Liadan closed her mouth on the retort she'd been going to make. Suddenly the air in the room seemed thick and heavy, and, disturbingly, she felt as if she was melting into the mattress beneath her. Unconsciously wetting her lips, she raised her big blue eyes nervously to meet Adrian's penetrating gaze. 'My hair isn't red. My mother said the colour was more like strawberry blonde.'

'Or red-gold...like autumn leaves.'

'That's the writer in you.'

'No, Liadan.' Adrian's voice was husky, his smile dangerously seductive. 'That's the man in me.'

The day **Maggie Cox** saw the film version of *Wuthering Heights,* with a beautiful Merle Oberon and a very handsome Laurence Olivier, was the day that she became hooked on romance. From that day onwards she spent a lot of time dreaming up her own romances, secretly hoping that one day she might become published and get paid for doing what she loves most! Now that her dream is being realised, she wakes up every morning and counts her blessings. She is married to a gorgeous man, and is the mother of two wonderful sons. Her two other great passions in life—besides her family and reading/writing—are music and films.

Recent titles by the same author:

THE WEALTHY MAN'S WAITRESS
A VERY PASSIONATE MAN
IN HER BOSS'S BED
A CONVENIENT MARRIAGE

HIS LIVE-IN MISTRESS

BY

MAGGIE COX

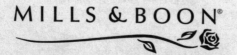

MILLS & BOON®

First published in Great Britain 2005
Harlequin Mills & Boon Limited,
Eton House, 18-24 Paradise Road, Richmond, Surrey TW9 1SR

© Maggie Cox 2005

ISBN 0 263 84130 8

Set in Times Roman 10½ on 12 pt.
01-0305-49976

Printed and bound in Spain
by Litografia Rosés, S.A., Barcelona

CHAPTER ONE

As HER new boots crunched against the thick snow that covered the sweeping yew-lined walk leading to the house Liadan was struck by the beauty and grandeur of the dramatic, imposing edifice that rose up before her. She stopped for a moment to take it in. Draped in a glistening white mantle of snow, its forbidding stone exterior with four rows of perfectly symmetrical eighteenth-century windows gazed down imperiously at her approach, as if questioning her right to be there. For the first time since she'd decided to answer the ad she'd circled so hopefully in the local paper, Liadan experienced a small but impossible-to-ignore shiver of doubt.

Was she doing the right thing? Was she even capable of undertaking the role of housekeeper in such a large and awe-inspiring dwelling? This was vastly different from her parents' mid-size but manageable little hotel in Dorset.

Sighing a breath that immediately turned to steam in the cold, Liadan tried hard to banish her doubts and instead concentrated on putting her best foot forward and continuing her journey towards the house with a much more optimistic gait.

When she lifted the huge iron knocker, letting it fall twice against the grand double-doored entrance, the sound intruded on the chill frozen air like a drunken visitor blundering in on a wake. A flock of birds calmly nesting in a nearby denuded oak flew into the air in an indignant flurry of surprise, their combined chirruping echoing eerily in the dense winter landscape. Wrapping her orange wool scarf more securely around the collar of her long tweed coat, Liadan couldn't help biting down on her lip as her imagination briefly ran wild, and she wondered if some haughty grey-haired butler would open the door and arrogantly instruct her to go round to the tradesman's entrance. Her sense of humour surfacing, she allowed herself a tentative smile at the thought.

In fact the person who answered was a slim brunette, probably in her early forties, dressed attractively in jeans and a red polo-necked sweater. The woman extended her hand in welcome without hesitation.

'You must be Liadan? Hello there, I'm Kate Broomfield. We spoke on the phone.'

The friendly voice she recalled from her telephone inquiry just two days ago didn't disappoint now that Liadan came face to face with its owner, and her relief was palpable.

'Pleased to meet you. Gosh, it's cold out there!' She grasped Kate's outstretched hand firmly with equal warmth. Relaxing, Liadan let her blue-eyed gaze wander round the large, imposing entrance hall she was invited into, her heartbeat quickening at the sight of the huge lofty ceilings with their grand antique brass chandeliers and candle sconces on the walls.

'I didn't see a car. Where did you park?' Kate enquired, watching as the younger woman removed her orange woollen gloves and slipped open the top button of her coat. The hall was surprisingly warm for such a vast area.

'I didn't come by car. I walked up from the village.'

'You're brave in this weather! That's a long walk.' Kate smiled, her brown eyes approving. 'But of course you're a local girl, aren't you? Though you do realise this is a living-in position? Mr Jacobs insists on that.'

'I know. It's not a problem.' For a moment Liadan tried to absorb the full implications of living in such a grand if somewhat remote house, her heart sinking a little at the idea of leaving her cosy little cottage behind. But then that was the beauty of being local. On her afternoons off she could go back home and see to anything that needed doing in her absence. Maybe after a while, when she got to know her employer better, he might even let her have the odd night off so that she could sleep in her own perfectly comfortable bed and play her piano? Not to mention make a fuss of her cat, Izzy. As it was, she would miss not being able to do all those things whenever she felt like it. But as long as her neighbour Jack fed the cat and gave her a little attention now and again to make up for Liadan not being there, she would manage just fine.

Right now, all that was supposition. She hadn't secured the job yet and might not if she didn't look sharp. The ad had specified someone between the ages of thirty-five and fifty, and Liadan was twenty-seven. Kate had told her not to worry too much about that. If she proved to be the right person for the job, Mr Jacobs would waive the age restriction, in Kate's opinion.

'Want a cup of coffee before I take you in to meet Adrian?'

'Adrian?'

'Mr Jacobs. Initially he'll probably insist you address him more formally, but after a while no doubt you'll be calling him Adrian too.'

As much as she loved the idea of a warming drink to thaw her out, Liadan felt she'd much rather get the interview over and done with first. He might take one

look at her and decide she was far too young for the
job of housekeeper of such a grand old house, she
thought anxiously. But she had grown up helping her
parents run a very successful small hotel and she was
no stranger to hard work and long back-breaking
hours—especially after her father had died and it had
been just her and her mother.

'If you don't mind, I'd rather meet Mr Jacobs first.
Have you had many other applicants for the job?'

'We've seen two before you but they were both completely wrong. Follow me. He's doing paperwork this
morning so he won't be in the best of moods, I warn
you. But don't let that put you off. He's a fair employer
and the pay is good, as no doubt you've noticed.'

Liadan had. It was the main reason she had applied
for the job in the first place. That and the fact it was
actually local to where she lived. But she couldn't help
wondering what had been so wrong about her two pre-
decessors...

Smiling reassuringly, Kate rapped smartly on the set
of dark oak double doors at the end of a cavernous
hallway carpeted in faded red and gold, then swept in
ahead of Liadan as a deep voice answered, 'Come!'

Her heart tripping as Kate announced her, Liadan
followed more slowly behind the brunette. Her gaze
settled with a little shiver of shock on the man seated
behind an old-fashioned writing bureau, his long jeans-
clad legs stuck out in front of him as he perused what
looked to be a letter. When he glanced up to examine
her as she stood beside Kate, the dark, almost black
eyes were about as cold and as frozen as Liadan's toes
inside her boots. Somehow, meeting those eyes, Liadan
no longer felt so confident about applying for this job.

Adrian Jacobs had a gaze that would freeze out the sun, and that had to be worrying.

'So you are Miss Willow?' There was a slight, amused tug of his well-shaped but stern mouth that made Liadan's stomach roll over. 'What kind of a name is that?'

Her shoulders stiffened. 'What do you mean?'

'Did you make it up? Is it some kind of pseudonym or something?'

'No, I didn't make it up and it's not a pseudonym. My name is my name and that's all I can tell you.' Just who did he think he was, making fun of her name? Liadan was experiencing some very strong doubts about the interview progressing much further after such a prickly and unpromising start. But she forced herself to stay calm and decided the best approach was not to take his comment personally. 'At school they used to call me "willow tree". There were some children who had to suffer far worse nicknames than that, so I guess I got off lightly.'

'Hmm.' Glancing back at his letter, he put it down on the desk with a sigh, rubbing at his temples as he did so. Then, as if coming to a decision, he turned to face her more squarely. Once again Liadan's heart missed a beat. His nose was too big, his eyes hooded and his mouth far too severe to suggest that it ever smiled much. And yet with his thick black hair streaked with fine grey strands here and there and the undoubted hint of muscle beneath his dark sweater, his sheer God-given maleness suggested an impression of great strength and indomitability that was quite awesome.

'You seem a little young to be seeking employment as a housekeeper. How old are you exactly, Miss *Willow*?'

Was her age going to be a strike against her...as well as her name, apparently? Flicking open a second and third button on her coat, Liadan told herself to remain calm. With a big fire blazing in the huge stone fireplace, the heat was definitely beginning to permeate her several layers of winter clothing. 'I'm twenty-seven but please don't let that put you off, Mr Jacobs. I've had several years of experience in housekeeping, helping my parents run a busy hotel in Dorset. Hard work doesn't faze me and I've done most things, from cooking three-course meals to mending a fuse and plumbing in a washing machine. Most of all, I'm cheerful to be around and I'm very willing.'

'Willing?' Mr Jacobs' darkly forbidding brows came together in a sardonic little frown.

Colouring, Liadan smiled. 'Helpful. I meant helpful.'

'Of course you did. What about a boyfriend, Miss Willow? Do you have one and won't he miss you if you come to work here?'

Guessing that he would probably laugh out loud if she told him that her year-long engagement to Michael Marston had broken off because he'd decided to join the priesthood, Liadan shook her head slowly, garnering every ounce of courage she possessed to ride this particular storm.

'No, Mr Jacobs. I don't have a boyfriend.'

'So there's no problem with you living in?'

'None whatsoever.'

'Liadan lives in the village, Adrian,' Kate piped up. 'She's a local girl.'

'She's too young and probably won't last the week.' His assessment was swiftly damning, and Liadan's hackles rose with indignation at such a scathing dismissal. Biting her lip, she was nonetheless determined to hold her ground.

'Mr Jacobs, if you'll just hear me out, I—'

'I don't employ any other staff in the house, Miss Willow. Could you handle the isolation?'

Isolation didn't faze Liadan. Nor did loneliness. A person could survive both of those states and still have a reasonably fulfilling life. Besides, she liked her own company. She'd never found being on her own a punishment as some of her friends did.

'I live alone anyway. I'm used to my own company,' she answered him.

'Good. After the two disappointing alternatives I interviewed earlier, perhaps you're more suitable than you look. So how soon can you start? Kate is leaving for London tomorrow and I need to have someone in place before she goes.'

Was he offering her the job? Blinking at him, Liadan stared in disbelief. After his previous comment about her being too young she'd more or less convinced herself that he would show her the door. 'Um, as soon as you need me to, I should think,' she replied a little breathlessly.

'What about references—do you have any?'

She started to delve into her bag for the two letters of recommendation she'd brought. One from her mother, bless her, in her former capacity as hotel proprietor; the other from Moonbeams, the little esoteric shop where she had worked for the past three years until it had gone bust six weeks ago.

Adrian put up his hand as if to stop her. 'Leave them with Kate. She'll show you to your room, then give you a tour of the house and a list of daily duties. I desire trust and discretion at all times, Miss Willow. I don't like being disturbed unduly, but I do expect you to be on call whenever I need you. You'll have one afternoon off a week as well as every other weekend off. The remuneration I'm sure you already know. That's all. I'll leave her in your capable hands, Kate. And how about some coffee when you're ready?'

'I'll bring you some when I've shown Liadan her room.' Kate smiled at her.

'Good.' Head down, he was already preoccupied with the contents of his letter before the two women reached the door.

Kate told her he was a writer. A very successful author of crime thrillers, writing under the pen name of Alexander Jacobsen. Once a highly successful journalist reporting on international conflicts all around the globe, he'd had the respect of his peers and the public alike during his career in news. Liadan experienced a shock wave of recognition at the news. Somewhere in the misty annals of her mind, she'd vaguely heard of Adrian Jacobs, but Alexander Jacobsen was the name that resonated. His hard-hitting crime novels always got to number one on the bestseller lists. Although that particular genre definitely did not appeal to her taste, her brother Callum had lent her a couple one Christmas and she had been unable to put them down, they were so gripping. If rather dark. Was that a legacy from some of the terrible atrocities he must have witnessed in his previous career? The thought made her shudder.

'Occasionally we get the odd reporter or two trying to infiltrate their way into the house,' Kate continued, 'but one thing you should be aware of is that Adrian absolutely never, under no circumstances, gives interviews. I would ask that you respect his privacy and don't divulge any personal information to anyone, and certainly nobody from the village. He's been gossiped about enough in the past and he doesn't need the heartache. Do a good job and obey those rules and you two will get on like a house on fire.'

That was the point where Liadan parted company with Kate's views. One only had to spend a couple of minutes in the same room with the man to realise he was not exactly brimming over with the warmth of human kindness. Instinctively Liadan knew their relationship would be a challenging one. Still, that didn't bother her too much. She was here to do a job, a job that would pay her more than enough money to live on and maintain her beloved little cottage in the village. More than that, she dared not hope for.

Once upon a time she had longed to meet a wonderful man and have children, but now that longing had been undeniably tarnished. Having spent an intense eighteen months in a relationship with a man whose spiritual conflicts had precluded him from having an intimate relationship with his fiancée, and who'd viewed her work in an esoteric bookshop as close to 'communing with the devil', she was in no hurry to repeat the exercise. Being with Michael had all but sucked Liadan dry emotionally. She had mistaken initially strong feelings of friendship for love, and no sacrifice she'd made had been enough as far as Michael had been concerned.

But that was then. Right now all she wanted to do was put the past firmly behind her and carve out a new destiny for herself.

The following morning as she unpacked and hung her clothes in the big oak wardrobe in her room, she paused to glance out of the window at the picturesque winter scene before her. The snow had completely passed Christmas by, but now, in early January, the heavens had suddenly opened and covered everything in a perfect coating of white frosting. Briefly wondering how her new employer had spent the holiday season—had he celebrated at home with friends and family?—Liadan reflected on her own solitary Christmas, just herself and Izzy. Granted, it had been by choice. She hadn't felt like flying out to Spain to join her mother and her new man, and after the traumatic break-up with Michael had not wanted to inflict her less-than-cheerful mood on her brother or her friends. No. She had definitely done the right thing spending the season on her own.

'Liadan, can you come down to the kitchen as soon as you've finished unpacking?'

Opening the door, she found Kate Broomfield on the other side of it, her cheeks pink as if she'd been rushing. 'Of course.'

'I want to go over everything with you. I've made lists but you might want to make some notes of your own as back-up. We'll have a cup of tea and a chat and I'll fill you in on anything you want to know. Ten minutes' time okay with you?' Peering over Liadan's shoulder, she noted the neatly folded clothing on the big brass bed and the opened doors of the large oak wardrobe.

Liadan nodded. 'I've nearly finished.'

'Good. Sorry everything's such a mad rush but I'm due to catch a train in just under two hours. I've been telling Adrian he needed to interview people for the past three months but would he listen? That's Adrian for you! Once he's in work mode he's on another planet. Anyway, you're here now, and, if you ask me, he's definitely made the right choice. Somebody young like you will be a breath of fresh air for him. See you in a tick, then.' And with that, she turned and hurried down the corridor.

Watching Kate depart just a short while later, Liadan felt as nervous as a new mother bringing her baby home from the hospital for the first time. From now on the welfare of this amazing house and its master was *her* responsibility. The thought made her stomach plummet and for a long moment she seriously pondered if she'd taken on much more than she was capable of handling. She hadn't set eyes on Adrian Jacobs since her interview yesterday and, as much as she'd like to, couldn't put off seeing him any longer. He and Kate had presumably said their goodbyes privately before Kate had come to find Liadan to tell her she was going. Now, standing alone in the huge entrance hall, the house suddenly covered in a blanket of silence since the other woman's cheery goodbye, Liadan glanced down at her watch and psyched herself up to take her new employer a cup of coffee. At least it would give her an excuse to break the ice a little with him since her abrupt interview yesterday. Making up her mind to do just that, she went to the kitchen, thankful for the warmth that greeted her as she entered, and, placing the kettle on the Aga, sought out a matching cup and saucer.

Minutes later, cup of coffee and a plate of digestive biscuits arranged on a tray, Liadan took a deep breath outside the doors of Adrian's study and knocked twice, smartly. At the terse, 'Come!' she pushed open the door and went inside.

Paper was strewn all around the floor at his feet. His black hair looked as if he had been dragging his fingers through it for the past half an hour at least, and her new employer's darkening expression leached every ounce of confidence from Liadan's bones and left her legs feeling as weak as a newborn lamb's.

'What is it?'

Trying to ignore the thumping of her heart, Liadan made herself smile and walk towards him. 'I thought you might like some coffee,' she said brightly, hoping he wouldn't register the slight quaver in her voice.

'Put the tray down on top of the piano and for God's sake don't put your feet anywhere near my papers!'

Adrian watched his new housekeeper do as he commanded. The rather old-fashioned long tweed skirt that adorned her slim figure was surprisingly complimentary to the thick wool orange, red and brown cowl-necked sweater she'd matched it with. Now she was free of the encumbrance of her winter coat and thick scarf, he registered that her hair was the same fiery red-gold as autumn leaves and it rippled down past her shoulders to her waist in eye-catching waves. Somewhere in Adrian's subconscious a deliberately buried memory tugged, and his stomach clenched tight in reflex as pain washed over him.

'Do you always wear your hair loose like that?' he asked gruffly.

Her hands gripping the edges of the tray as she settled it carefully on top of the gleaming ebony surface of the beautiful grand piano, Liadan turned her head in surprise. 'Mostly' she admitted, with a little shrug. 'Except when I'm working, of course.'

'Aren't you working now, Miss Willow? Or has that particular little fact somehow escaped you?'

Seeing the faint flush beneath her pale cheeks, Adrian felt equal measures of frustration and annoyance that the girl was so pretty. With her big blue eyes and china doll face she was a heartbreaker, all right. What had he been thinking of, offering this fragile-looking beauty the job that was most essential to his own well-being? He needed someone reliable, trustworthy and efficient, like Kate, not someone who looked as if she'd be crushed by just the sound of a harshly raised voice.

Damn it all to hell and back! Why had Kate left him in the lurch in the middle of his most ambitious project to date? He didn't want to be plagued with questions and inquiries from someone still wet behind the ears when he was working. After four and a half years, Kate knew practically all of his little foibles and idiosyncrasies, including his preferences when it came to the way he liked to work—not to mention food, music and reading material: the four essentials to make his life run smoothly, as far as Adrian was concerned. He didn't have time to break in a new housekeeper.

'I'll go up to my room and tie it back.' Liadan stepped back stiffly from the piano and turned towards him. The flush on her cheeks was no longer in evidence and her chin was raised a little, as if determined he wasn't going to bait her. She was annoyed, and, if his own present level of irritation continued, Adrian knew he would have only himself to blame when the girl threw in the towel and left him high and dry. At this moment, the prospect didn't seem too worrying.

'Before I go, I wondered if you had a preference for dinner? Kate's left me a list of options.'

'If she's left you a list of options, then pick one for me, Miss Willow. I don't have time to immerse myself in menu discussions when I'm in the middle of work.'

'Well, I—'

'If that's all you wanted to know, I trust you can now leave me in peace so that I can get on?'

Liadan wondered how she made it to the door without giving him a piece of her mind. The man had no manners as far as she could see, his superior, self-important tone rankled, and if she didn't need this job so badly in order to keep her little house she wouldn't hesitate to let him know in detail just what he could do with it! He hadn't even thanked her for the coffee, let alone asked her if she was settling in all right.

Two hours later, having completed a thorough vacuuming of the upstairs rooms on the first floor, excluding the room that Kate had pointed out as Adrian's— apparently that was to be cleaned once a week on a Thursday morning when Adrian generally went into town—Liadan returned to the kitchen to browse the recipe books Kate had left. Sipping a cup of camomile tea, her concentration on the list of ingredients needed to make the dish she had selected, she didn't realise Adrian had stepped into the room until he spoke.

'Taking a break already, Miss Willow?'

For a moment she stared into those chilly dark eyes in mute astonishment, then, when she'd gathered her wits, she pushed back a coiling strand of red-gold hair that had escaped from her hastily erected bun and frowned. 'I'm organising what I need for tonight's dinner, Mr Jacobs. Isn't that what you hired me for?'

'As long as you're not being idle. This is a big house and it takes a lot of looking after. *I* take a lot of looking after.'

Was he being facetious? Liadan really couldn't tell. Especially when his expression was about as impenetrable as the vaults of the Bank of England. Releasing a small sigh, she prayed he wasn't always going to be this difficult, this *provoking*. Had the affable and dependable Kate been subject to his arrogant moods immediately when she started to work for him? If she had, the woman surely deserved some kind of endurance medal for her troubles.

'What is it you want, Mr Jacobs? If you'll just tell me I'll see if I can help.'

What Adrian could have done with was a long hot bath followed by a massage. He'd been up most of the night writing, his shoulders ached, his head throbbed and he was irritated and angry at Kate's desertion. And all because the silly woman had fallen for some probably extremely dull professor of history her father had introduced her to during the summer holidays. He'd clearly misjudged her character, because he would have sworn she wasn't the type to fall head over heels in love like some giddy sixteen-year-old.

Reining in his thoughts on the matter, Adrian met Liadan's apprehensive blue gaze with a deep frown. He almost had the urge to ask her to oblige him with a massage just for the hell of it. She'd probably turn tail and run out of there so fast her feet would leave a trail of smoke in her wake. He would have smiled at the thought if the consequences of such an action wouldn't leave him in the direst straits possible.

'Right now I need to walk and think. Did Kate show you around the grounds when she took you on her little tour?'

'She would have done but she was in a hurry to catch her train.' Rising to her feet, Liadan folded her arms across her thick wool sweater for protection. Adrian Jacobs made her uneasy. He had a way of looking at her that made her feel as if he knew everything and she knew nothing—a trait that hardly boded well for a smooth association.

'Then go and put your coat on and come and join me. I'll point out a couple of things of interest but otherwise I'd prefer not to have any conversation. If you can manage to stay quiet I think I could tolerate some company for half an hour.'

Embarrassed heat scorching her cheeks, Liadan glanced down at the clean pine table with her thoughts rioting, wondering how she managed to refrain from picking up her cup of camomile tea and throwing it at him. Of all the unbelievably rude, *insufferable*— 'I'd rather stay here, if you don't mind. I really need to get my ingredients together to cook dinner.'

Jerking his head in annoyance, Adrian held Liadan riveted to the spot with the force of his steely-eyed stare. 'Go and get your coat, Miss Willow. When I said I could tolerate some company, I wasn't giving you the option of a refusal.'

CHAPTER TWO

THE air was so cold Liadan's breath practically turned to ice as soon as it left her lips. With her coat collar turned up high over her thick woollen scarf, she trailed behind Adrian as he strode ahead, his shoes crunching into the deep impacted snow and his gloveless hands buried deep inside the pockets of his long black coat. The sky was so white it almost matched the snow in brightness and Liadan wished she had her sunglasses to fend off the glare. Shielding her gaze with her gloved hand, she was deeply stirred by the magical landscape that revealed itself to her. Once she could simply accept that Adrian Jacobs wasn't going to be the most sociable or approachable boss she could hope for, then she could actually start to enjoy the wintry beauty of her incredible surroundings and take pleasure in it, she decided.

'That tower over there is two hundred and fifty years old and the clipped Holm oaks survive from the original garden. Just beyond the oaks there's an orangery and an ornamental stream.'

Adrian waited for Liadan to catch up with him as he turned and spoke, his breath mimicking little puffs of locomotive steam in the frosty afternoon air. Surprised by his unexpected solicitude, Liadan duly quickened her stride, her boots plunging deep into the snow as she struggled to find some kind of rhythm, all the while far too conscious of his steady dark gaze on her efforts.

'Gardens like this must take a lot of looking after,'

she breathed as she drew level. 'You must have a team of gardeners, surely?'

His dark eyes narrowed. 'Just George and his son Steven. They're here most days. You'll probably see them around. I don't tolerate too many people on my property, Miss Willow. On the whole, I find people demand far more than I wish to give.'

'But this is such a beautiful place. Don't you ever feel like sharing it?' The question was out before Liadan gave herself a chance to consider the wisdom of speaking such thoughts out loud. It hung suspended in the frozen air, making her squirm inside when it appeared that Adrian had not the slightest intention of answering her. But he didn't turn away and continue striding ahead as she expected. Instead, a deep scowl etching his brow, he folded his arms across his chest and stared at her.

'The answer to your question is no, Miss Willow. I expressly *don't* feel like sharing my home with anyone. I live here because I actively enjoy the isolation. My uncle lived here on his own for twenty-five years after his wife died. Accidents or illness permitting, I plan to do the same.'

Well, she'd wanted an answer and she'd got one. Did he have any idea how cold and lonely a proposition his words suggested? What had happened to the man that he preferred to live his life away from the rest of humanity, like some kind of eccentric, wealthy recluse?

'So you inherited the house from your uncle?' she asked.

'You were wondering how I could possibly afford to live in such grandeur on the pay of a jobbing writer,' Adrian drawled scathingly.

Liadan couldn't help but smile. 'I know you're a

very successful author of crime novels, Mr Jacobs. It's rare that your books *aren't* on the best-seller lists.'

'You've read my work?' A new expression stole into those impenetrable dark eyes of his. Surprise? Caution? Disbelief? Perhaps all three? Liadan couldn't be certain.

'My brother Callum is a fan. He lent me a couple of your books one Christmas when I had nothing else to read.' Colouring slightly at the admission and painfully aware that she could have chosen her words more carefully, she pressed on regardless before he could interrupt her. 'They were very intriguing.'

'But?'

To her consternation she saw that Adrian was smiling—well, for a second or two it seemed that the corners of his stern mouth lifted a little. Ducking her chin down into the warmth of her orange scarf, Liadan bravely met his questioning gaze. 'They were so…so dark and spine-chilling. And the endings were unredeemingly bleak.'

'So you were looking for some kind of redemption in my stories, were you? Some kind of light at the end of the tunnel to reassure you that really life couldn't be as bad as all that, and all's well that ends well?'

Her toes curling stiffly inside her boots, Liadan was beginning to wish she'd said nothing. Adrian's scornful tone made her opinions sound naïve and somehow uneducated, and just for a moment she hated him for that.

'Life *isn't* all bad, no matter what you say. Everyone has their tough times but we learn from them, don't we? We learn from them and move on. And things always get better as long as we don't give up, don't you agree?'

Her blue eyes sparkled a little defiantly, her words

stirring such a surprising feeling of rage inside Adrian's chest that he spun away from her before he said things he would probably only regret later. So the earnest Miss Willow thought that life was full of redeeming qualities, did she? How long before fate snatched the blinkers from her eyes and dealt her a crushing blow, one of the magnitude that he had suffered, to disabuse her of such an opinion?

As he strode far ahead, instinctively knowing she would have trouble keeping up with him, Adrian cursed himself for having the very thought that she might ever suffer such a tragedy.

The dining room was cold and cheerless, and as she laid a place setting for one at the head of the long oak refectory table that evening Liadan glanced distractedly at the empty fireplace, cursing herself for not thinking of laying a fire earlier. Even though the three radiators were switched to a high heat, the warmth they generated barely made an impact on the huge, draughty room. Those stately Georgian windows were the culprits. With their single-paned glass that the wind seemed to rattle through, no wonder the room remained chilled. Rubbing her hands together briskly to make them warmer, Liadan turned on her heel to return to the big bright kitchen, which would be cosily warm and full of fragrant cooking smells from the lamb casserole she'd put in the oven two hours ago. Distracted, she walked straight into a wall of steel with strong arms that immediately reached out to steady her as her eyes flew wide in shock.

'Mr Jacobs! I'm so sorry. I didn't see you there.'

'Where's the fire?'

Flustered, Liadan stepped back in dismay, glancing

over her shoulder at the empty grate, trying to convince herself that contact with his body hadn't sent shock waves of acute awareness flooding through her that made all her nerve endings sizzle. 'I'm afraid I forgot to lay it. I was so busy organising dinner I—'

'The question wasn't literal. I wondered where you were rushing off to in such a hurry.' A glint of amusement lurked in the dark depths of his fascinating eyes. Adrian's acute study of her was agonising, making her blood heat to an alarming degree.

'I was—I was anxious to see to dinner. Are you sure you want to eat in here? It's much warmer in the kitchen if you don't mind the cooking smells.'

'I always have my evening meal in the dining room—unless of course I'm working. Then I have it in my study.'

About to boldly suggest he do something radical and break the habit of a lifetime, Liadan clamped her mouth closed just in time and said nothing. So as well as dour and unfriendly he was a creature of habit too? The observation surprised her. In her mind, people who feared change feared life. But Adrian had reported back from some of the most inhospitable environs in the world—in some of the most dangerous situations. It didn't seem likely that a little thing like changing his dinnertime routine would faze him. Still, it annoyed her not to know the reason why he seemed such a stickler for routine.

'I'm just sorry it's so cold in here.' Subconsciously illustrating the fact by rubbing her hands up and down her arms in her thick wool sweater, Liadan ventured a smile.

'I think I have enough flesh covering my bones not

to be too bothered by the lowered temperatures, Miss Willow.'

Although his manner was teasing, there was no humour reflected in his hypnotically compelling face. Confronted with yet another reminder of that disturbingly hard male body, the muscles in his arms like ropes of steel if his earlier grip had been any indication, Liadan quickly averted her gaze in case her fascinated expression gave her away.

'Well, then... I'll bring in your meal if you'd like to sit down.'

'Bring some wine too. I trust Kate left you instructions as to my preferences?'

A dark full-bodied red with dinner. Liadan didn't know why the description should bother her so, but right at that moment it did.

'Right,' she said, hovering at the door. Paying her no further attention, Adrian moved to the head of the table and sat down.

Her perfume lingered when she'd gone. Not overpowering, but light and sweet where it drifted on the air like May blossom. Breathing it in and feeling its unsettling effect, Adrian picked up his empty wineglass and flicked it restlessly with his nail. Kate hadn't worn perfume—at least, not that he remembered. Could he enforce a rule that the wearing of perfume was banned whenever he was around, on the grounds that it was far too distracting for his peace of mind? He could just imagine what his pretty new housekeeper would think about that. No doubt she already saw him as a younger version of Scrooge. But why should he worry when, if his initial assumption proved to be right, she wouldn't even last the week? Irritably he put down the wineglass. Then folding his arms across his chest, he leant back against the high-backed dining chair and briefly shut his eyes.

Nicole had always worn perfume. Even in the most unsuitable places, including the jungle. She used to laugh that a girl had standards to maintain and should never forget her femininity... The thought stole up on him like a thief in the night, searing his chest like a firebrand, and he sat bolt upright, grasping the edges of the table for support. That was twice in one day he'd thought about Nicole—the woman he'd planned to marry, fellow journalist and love of his life. Months had gone by without him allowing such thoughts access to even the merest dusty corner of his mind, and now twice in the space of less than twelve hours her memory had hit him hard, like a fierce blow slamming into his ribcage that doubled him up in agony. His mind's eye saw her: glorious red-gold hair splayed out on that sun-baked concrete, blood staining the silken strands like some vile desecration; her beautiful green eyes staring up at Adrian in confusion and pain as she drew her last few breaths on this earth.

The news team had been warned about a possible attack on the embassy for weeks leading up to the terrorist bomb that had blown it to smithereens. But on that baking-hot day, after they'd travelled for three days to get there through notorious bandit country, Adrian's belief in his own invincibility had been sky-high. So much so that he'd convinced the other, less confident members of his crew that, as long as they kept their wits about them at all times, all would be well. Seconds before they started to walk into the embassy, he'd been sharing a joke with Nicole about the unappetising rations they'd endured the last few days, when Mark, one of the older, more experienced cameramen on the team, had called him back to the Jeep to fetch the micro-cassette recorder he had left behind. Just as Adrian had reached the hot, mud-splattered vehicle all hell had broken loose, in an ear-splitting explosion that had sounded like the end of the world. Mark had shoved him roughly to the ground to give him some cover and Adrian had stared helplessly across to the sidewalk to see Nicole lying there...

'I wonder if any more snow will fall during the night.'

'What?' Staring distractedly up into Liadan's guileless blue gaze, Adrian forced his attention abruptly back to the present. Watching her small, pale hand steadily pour the ruby-red wine into his empty glass, he stole a second or two to wipe away the perspiration that he knew beaded his brow.

'I said, I wonder if it will snow again tonight?' Smiling, she put down the bottle, then adjusted his place-mat so that it sat more squarely on the table.

'I have many interests but predicting the weather isn't one of them.'

In less than a second, his caustic comment had wiped the smile from her face as though it had never been. Seeing the hurt in her eyes, Adrian took a deep slug of wine, remaining stubbornly silent as she mumbled, 'Excuse me,' and retreated from the room without another word.

It was with relief that Liadan turned down the perfectly white linen and pretty red and white quilt on her bed that night. Shivering as she removed her robe, she slid between the ice-cool sheets, making a mental note to go in search of a hot-water bottle the next morning, then pulled up the covers and sat back against the plumped up pillows with a pent-up sigh that she felt she'd been holding in all day. It had been a trying evening and one she wanted swiftly to forget. Adrian was right. Maybe she wouldn't last the week after all? He was certainly pushing her towards that inevitable conclusion with his morose, uncommunicative behaviour.

Who could blame her if she quit tomorrow, under the circumstances? Clearly the efficient Kate Broomfield had had a substantial advantage when it came to dealing with Adrian Jacobs. She'd had the experience and the wisdom of maturity on her side to help her cope. If not that, then the woman had to have possessed something special to endure four and half years at the beck and call of a man who didn't seem to view the rest of the human race as even remotely worthy of his attention.

Blinking at the clock on the nightstand, wishing she had more than just five short hours in which to get some sleep before rising at dawn to light the fire in Adrian's study and make breakfast, Liadan had to admit that her shorter working hours at the shop had perhaps made her a little soft. Now she would have to get used to rising at the crack of sparrows once again— just as she and her mother had done when they'd run the hotel together.

Thoughts of the family home brought thoughts of her father and, not willing to go down that melancholy road at this moment when she was already feeling vulnerable, Liadan determinedly pushed the thought away to save it for another time when she was more able to handle it. She wished that Izzy were here with her, curled up on her lap, her soft, mesmerising purr the only sound to distract her racing thoughts, instead of the unfamiliar creaks and groans of a venerable old house settling down for the night.

In the gentle glow of the lamplight, Liadan guided her gaze to systematically check every dark corner of the bedroom, which was too large and impersonal for her taste and reminded her of a room in a museum. Satisfied that there was nothing to spook her save her own too wild imagination, she promised herself that when next she got home she would fetch some things to make it more homely. There was a charming picture of a cottage garden that hung in her bedroom that always gave her comfort. Perhaps if she brought it back with her it might act as some kind of lucky charm? Right now she could do with some positive influences. She wasn't the sort who gave up easily but, if she should lose this job, such an opportunity to work so close to home and make some decent money to live on wasn't likely to show up again soon, no matter how optimistic she was.

There were two viable options as far as she could see. One was to make the best of a difficult situation, sit it out and pray that Adrian Jacobs had a more agreeable side than he had displayed so far, which would reveal itself to her in the fullness of time. The second was to try and make herself as indispensable as she could to her new employer—as indispensable as Kate had been, if that was even remotely possible.

Her eyes gritty with lack of sleep, Liadan was on her knees in the study making up the fire in the impressive marble grate when Adrian came into the room. His appearance disturbed her more than she cared to admit, and not just because she was unsure that she was up to the job of being his housekeeper. With that thick black hair streaked with grey touching his collar, broadly muscular shoulders and a visage that was far more sexy than handsome, he had an aura of power and authority about him that would make a person sit up and take notice, whether they wanted to or not. No doubt it had come in very handy in all those threatening terrains he had reported from, back when he was a journalist, Liadan mused. But such authority first thing in the morning made her feel at a distinct disadvantage. She knew she wasn't at her best after an almost completely sleepless night and she had only herself to blame. She'd let her anxiety about the job, about Adrian and about being attracted to emotionally unavailable men like Michael nearly drive her crazy.

'Good morning.'

Her heart almost stopped at his greeting, her thoughts reflecting how good he looked in black, how imposing and how…ticked off.

'Mr Jacobs, I was just about to—'

'The fire should have been lit in here at least half an hour ago, Miss Willow. I thought Kate made my routine clear? And where is my coffee? I went into the kitchen but unless my eyesight is failing me I saw no evidence of any being made, not a drop. Care to explain why?'

Hearing the unsettled throb of her own heartbeat in her ears, Liadan sat back on her haunches and nervously pushed her fringe from her eyes.

'Kate told me she usually gets up around five-thirty, Mr Jacobs, which I *did*. If it's taking me a little longer to build up the fire it's just that I'm a bit out of practice. Bear with me and you'll have your fire *and* your coffee in just a few more minutes' time.'

Amazed at her own ability to appear outwardly calm when inside she was seething at his criticism, Liadan turned her back on him once more to continue with the task in hand. She leant forward to set a match to the tinder, her hand shaking, her face growing hotter by the second at the idea that Adrian's eyes were burning into the back of her head. She knew she was a good and reliable worker but somehow, from the minute she'd started to work for this man, she had managed to appear anything but. Still, she was resolved to see it through no matter how tough it got, and she vowed to talk to him just as soon as she got the chance to try and set a few things straight before the situation went from bad to worse. It wasn't unreasonable of him to expect certain standards, but, in Liadan's book, it *was* unreasonable to speak to an employee in such an arrogant, rude and high-handed way that it made them feel like leaving. What was wrong with the man, for goodness' sake? Was he this hostile to everyone or had something about her personally rubbed him up the wrong way?

'I'll put the coffee on myself while you see to the fire,' he said from behind her. 'But don't take too long. I'd like my breakfast before I start work and I've got a busy day ahead of me.'

As he went out of the door Adrian could have sworn he heard Liadan mutter something heartfelt beneath her breath and he knew he probably deserved whatever insult she was currently castigating him with. If Kate knew how he was behaving towards his new housekeeper she'd read him the Riot Act, but didn't he have a right to expect good service when he'd made it perfectly clear that that was what he was looking for? As he walked back along the corridor to the kitchen he fought down a fresh resurgence of annoyance at Kate's desertion and told himself it was her fault entirely if his manner wasn't all that it should be. As for Liadan Willow—he'd better learn to keep his temper under strict control where she was concerned or he would quickly find himself without a housekeeper. It was that soft silken mass of red-gold hair of hers that was causing all the trouble. It reminded him of the one woman he had truly loved, stirring desperately agonising feelings of recrimination and regret about what had happened that dreadful day that would be with him for the rest of his life...

But his book was nearly finished. He couldn't risk being abandoned by his housekeeper now when he was at such a crucial point, so he would endeavour to be more civil towards her. Just two more weeks, he estimated, and the thing would be done. Perhaps then his mind would allow him a brief period of peace from the demons of creativity that drove him and he could think about something else besides work. But as he stood spooning dark roast coffee grounds into the percolator Adrian wondered with pain what else he had worth thinking about in his life besides work.

'Thanks for breakfast. I'm going to my study now, so please take any calls, would you? Just take messages for now and tell them I'll get back to them later.'

Pausing from stacking a newly washed plate on the drainer, Liadan turned to acknowledge him. Had she really heard him say 'please' and 'thank you' in one breath? At least she hadn't messed up the breakfast. She'd served him up eggs and bacon and tomatoes done to perfection, she'd kept the toast hot and the coffee strong as he liked it and the food had certainly seemed to lighten his mood.

'Okay.'

'Oh, and Liadan?'

She went still as a statue at his unexpected use of her name. 'Yes?'

'I need you to go and find George Ferrers, my head gardener. Tell him I'd like a meeting at nine sharp.'

'But where will I...?'

He'd gone from the room before she had a chance to finish her question. Throwing the dishcloth back into the sink full of hot, sudsy water, Liadan took a moment to gather her thoughts. She gazed out of the window, and experienced a sudden deep longing for the camaraderie and warmth of Moonbeams, the charmingly pretty little shop where she had worked for the past three years with two of the nicest workmates you could wish to find. It was evident so far that working for Adrian Jacobs would not be such a joy.

Wrapped up warm in her long tweed coat, her orange mohair scarf looped snugly round her neck, Liadan filled her lungs joyfully with deep breaths of crisp morning air as she strode out purposefully in search of George Ferrers. Instinctively she headed towards two large greenhouses she'd glimpsed yesterday on her brief tour of the gardens with Adrian. There was too much snow for anyone to do much in the garden, she decided, so it stood to reason if there were greenhouses, that was where she'd find the man she was looking for.

She put her head round the door of the first building, and her spirits lifted when she saw a tall, older man garbed in old trousers, wellingtons, a thick Arran sweater and a sheepskin jacket patting earth down into a huge earthenware pot. He tipped his cap back on his head when Liadan called out, 'Hello,' waiting silently for her to join him.

'You must be George,' she said smilingly, holding out her hand. He had a kind face, one you could trust, she silently assessed. 'I'm Liadan Willow. Mr Jacobs' new housekeeper.'

'If that's the case, then things are looking up around here in a *big* way,' drawled an interested male voice from behind her.

CHAPTER THREE

THE owner of the voice was tall and handsome, with jet-black hair and a diamond stud glistening in one ear-lobe. As he walked towards Liadan, his scruffy jeans hanging low on his hips, she noted with irritation that he had a deliberate swagger about him, telling her instantly that he imagined himself God's gift to women. She didn't normally take immediate dislikes, but she did to this man.

'And you are?'

'Steven. Steven Ferrers. George here is my dad.'

Deliberately redirecting her gaze to the older man, Liadan didn't miss the flash of disapproval in his light blue eyes over her shoulder at his son. 'What can I do for you, Miss Willow?'

'Mr Jacobs would like to see you at nine o'clock sharp, if that's okay? He asked me to come and tell you.'

'I expect it'll be about the snow piled up at the back door. Steven here was just about to get on to it, weren't you, son?'

'When I've finished the other hundred odd jobs I've already been ordered to do.' Not bothering to temper his obvious resentment, Steven leant back against a table full of trays of seedlings, making no secret of the fact that he was studying Liadan's figure with an insolence that made her furious. Biting back her indignation, Liadan found herself urgently needing to be back inside the house, ensconced in the warmth and safety of the kitchen, and tackling the list of jobs she had ahead of her for the day. Something about Steven Ferrers put her on edge and she decided that in future she would endeavour to keep contact with him to a strict minimum.

'Bit of a slave-driver, our Mr Jacobs. Don't you be letting him wear you out with all that housework, Miss Willow. Those pretty hands of yours were meant for finer things than pushing a vacuum cleaner around.'

Considering that her hands were still firmly inside her bright orange gloves, Liadan failed to see how he could judge them and was irked that a man she had only seconds before clapped eyes on made so free with his comments. George too, it seemed, had had his patience stretched beyond endurance. 'That's enough, Steven! Have you forgotten who pays your wages round here? You treat Mr Jacobs and anyone who works for him with respect, you hear?'

Turning to Liadan, he scratched his head briefly beneath his cap and shifted awkwardly from one foot to the other. 'I apologise for my son's behaviour, Miss Willow. He meant no harm, I'm sure, but he gets a little carried away sometimes. Please don't take offence.'

Feeling for the man's embarrassment, Liadan didn't hesitate to give him a reassuring smile. 'None taken, Mr Ferrers. Well… I'd better be getting back to the house. Work to do.'

'Be seeing you around, Miss Willow.' With a smirk on his face that Liadan longed to obliterate with a sharp slap, Steven Ferrers deliberately dropped his gaze to her chest before she turned and walked away. A shiver skating down her spine, she hurried out of the greenhouse, not pausing to glance back even once before reaching the steps of the main house.

'Come in and be quick about it!'

Her spine knotting with tension and her palms prickly with heat, Liadan pushed open the door of the study and entered the room with the tray of sandwiches and coffee she had brought for Adrian's lunch. If she'd hoped that the five-star breakfast she'd served him this morning had mellowed his mood, then she was obviously going to be disappointed judging by the scowl on his face. She'd taken such care with the sandwiches she'd made, too, cutting the bread into perfect triangles and decorating them with sprigs of parsley and slices of tomato. But he barely acknowledged her presence, too preoccupied with the papers strewn across his writing table, his black hair obviously ruffled by his restless fingers as he worked. 'Leave the tray on the piano,' he barked, and continued to work as though she were already gone.

Was she so wrong to expect some common courtesies from him, such as please and thank you? Liadan didn't think so. It seriously bothered her that he seemed to imagine that he was somehow outside the realms of what was considered polite for everyone else. But even though she was deeply annoyed by his ill manners, she couldn't pretend she wasn't aware of the distinct chill in the air and it wasn't just Adrian's icy demeanour that was the cause. The fire had all but gone out, leaving just the barest red glow in its dying embers. In all conscience, Liadan couldn't walk away without doing something about it.

'Where do you think you're going?' Adrian snapped

as she swept past his chair instead of heading for
the door.

'I thought I'd fix the fire. It's nearly out and it's
chilly in here. I'll try not to disturb you.'

Didn't she know that that was impossible? Adrian
thought with profound irritation. She was wearing that
fragrance again, the one that seemed to wind itself
round his senses and interrupt his train of thought like
some kind of confounded will-o'-the-wisp. It seemed
to mock and tease him, and tempt him to become far
more aware than was wise of the woman who wore it.
As if compelled, he lifted his gaze helplessly to her
hair, noting the soft but precarious bun she'd fashioned,
with a few silky red-gold tendrils floating loose to
frame her lovely face. She really had the prettiest cornflower-blue eyes he'd ever seen, Adrian realised. What
had he been thinking of, hiring such a looker for his
housekeeper? He'd told himself hiring her had been the
path of least resistance—Kate was leaving and he
couldn't interrupt his work to ring round agencies to
find other people to interview. She'd said she was hard-
working and for some reason Adrian had believed her.
She didn't look the type whose lips would lie easily.
But now he couldn't help wondering if he'd made a
serious mistake in taking her on.

It had been four and a half years since his disastrous
short-lived affair with Petra Collins—the one that had
hit the tabloid headlines and hastened his decision to
retreat from the world for a while. But clearly, if the
way his libido was acting up around Liadan was any
indication, he had been without a woman for too long.

'Leave it.'

'Why?' Her heart racing, because suddenly she
seemed to have his full and disturbing attention and

she was ill-prepared for it, Liadan came to an abrupt standstill.

'Because I'm working and I don't want to be disturbed any more than is strictly necessary! I can't have you clattering about in here while I'm trying to concentrate.'

'Clattering about?' Her cheeks growing pinker by the second as indignation cramped her throat, Liadan stared. 'I was concerned for your comfort, that's all. I wasn't trying to make a nuisance of myself. Have you any idea what the temperature is outside?'

'When I want a weather report I'll switch on the news.'

Tearing her gaze from his stony expression, Liadan headed straight for the double doors, her heart pounding so hard inside her chest that for a moment she was hardly aware of where she was, let alone her destination. 'Fine!' she burst out before she left. 'Freeze to death for all I care!'

Back in the kitchen, her appetite gone, she pushed away the small decorative sideplate with her sandwiches on to stare miserably down at the small bumps and grooves on the big pine table, willing herself to calm down. Just who did he think he was, speaking to her like that? They weren't back in the Middle Ages as far as she knew and she wasn't some serf to be bossed about at will, as if her life were not her own! It would serve him right if she walked out right this minute. See how he would cope if he had to do his own cooking and cleaning and make up fires! If there were any justice in the world he'd starve *and* get hypothermia very quickly...

She took her frustration out on the table and thumped it. Why did she have to recall just then that Michael had disliked it immensely when she lost her temper? It had pointed to a wild nature, in his opinion, one that he wasn't altogether certain he could handle. Liadan groaned. Michael had been wary of anything emotional that might tip the precarious balance of an existence where order and restraint were paramount, so obviously losing one's temper was a complete no-no. When he'd finally admitted he couldn't commit to Liadan because his faith was calling him in another direction, one that she couldn't be a part of, she'd been relieved but angry too. She'd long realised that the relationship hadn't been going anywhere but she'd stupidly put her own life on hold for eighteen months while Michael had wrestled with his own decisions about the future.

And then two months after the break-up—to add insult to injury—Liadan had learned that she no longer had a job because her employer had gone bankrupt. Now it looked as if she'd be unemployed again very soon…

'Liadan.'

Glancing up at her name, she rested her wary gaze on Adrian's tall, imposing figure in the doorway.

'What?' She steeled herself to hear the worst. Without a doubt he was going to give her her marching orders. The only consolation was that she would see her cat sooner than she'd anticipated and be able to make a fuss of her tonight. Oh, well… 'always look for the gift,' as Jennie, the owner of Moonbeams, had wisely counselled on more than one occasion.

'I'd be grateful if you'd come back into the study and make up the fire. You're right. It's bloody cold in there and even I can't type with frozen fingers.' He was smiling and suddenly Liadan found her breathing and her power of speech seriously impeded. Having the power of that smile trained on her was like diving for seashells and coming up with diamonds. Did the man have any idea how much that simple act humanised him? It made him seem much less like the coldly distant character she was getting used to and so much…dared she say it? *Warmer.*

'You're not going to fire me?'

'Now why would you think that?' Apparently bemused, Adrian leant his shoulder against the doorjamb as if the imperative to get back to work was no longer relevant.

'Because I lost my temper.' She heaved a sigh and Adrian's already engaged glance was drawn to the shapely swell of her breasts beneath her black ribbed sweater. Because her waist was so small, it highlighted her well-endowed chest, and, before he knew what he was about, Adrian imagined those same shapely breasts filling his palms. He imagined his thumbs brushing sensuously across her nipples, urging them to tight, hard, sexy peaks, and suddenly his vivid daydreaming led him into deep hot water when he found himself irrevocably and heavily aroused.

'As far as I'm aware that's hardly a sacking offence—particularly when I provoked it.' His desire had made his voice unwittingly smoky.

Unable to tear her gaze from his, Liadan urged herself to her feet, willing herself to wake up from the trance she seemed to be in.

'I'll go and see to the fire, then.'

Alarmed by the sudden, dangerously provocative turn of his thoughts, Adrian dropped his glance guiltily to the table, seeing the small plate of sandwiches she had made. 'Eat your lunch first. A few more minutes won't make much difference. Thank you, Liadan.' And with that, he was gone from the doorway before she even had a chance to reply.

Closing the curtains in her room, Liadan went suddenly rigid when she spied torchlight moving stealthily down the front steps towards the gardens. Adrian? She squinted hard to try and see. What was he doing out at this hour? The small old-fashioned clock on her mantelpiece had just struck midnight so it was a bit late for going for a walk, wasn't it? Shivering in her velour robe because the heating had gone off for the night, she quickly moved away from the window and glanced disconsolately at the thick, hard-backed biography on her bed. Right now, reading held no appeal whatsoever and she didn't feel much like sleeping, either. Astonishing when she considered how dog-tired she had been this morning. For some reason her whole body was restless, thrumming with energy and the need to expend it somehow.

If she was honest, she had been feeling that way since Adrian had smiled at her at lunchtime. His changes of mood were disconcerting and she didn't know whether to allow herself to believe he did possess a more amenable side after all, or whether he'd simply decided to make an effort in case Liadan decided staying wasn't worth the trouble. His work was obviously all-consuming—he wouldn't want to have to break off from it to start searching for a replacement housekeeper, no matter how disappointing his present one seemed. And yet… When all was said and done the man was definitely an enigma, and the main reason that Liadan couldn't sleep was that she was becoming more curious about her ill-tempered, good-looking employer than was probably wise.

* * *

Walking through the gardens, his feet sliding and crunching on the snow-covered earth, Adrian finally felt he could breathe unencumbered once more. It didn't matter how big the house was or how many rooms it had—at times like these he simply needed the unconfined space of the outside. Only then would the prickling discomfort in his chest ease and his ensuing panic start to subside. It had been that way ever since Nicole's death and after eight years he wasn't holding out much hope for a change. What made him furious was that he didn't seem to have any control over his claustrophobia. It wasn't as if he spent every day dwelling on the terrible event that had indelibly shaped his future, but still the condition seemed to descend on him out of the blue. His psychologist friend, Andrew, had told him he mustn't blame himself and had tried to teach him strategies for coping. But Adrian hadn't wanted strategies, or advice—no matter how well meant. He simply wanted the ability to turn back time: to sit in the Jeep for a few minutes longer with Nicole on that mercilessly hot day and prevent her from going anywhere near the embassy gates.

Turning in the dark to stare at the huge house in front of him, with just one or two lights on downstairs and one shining from the first floor—Liadan's room—Adrian knew he didn't really want to stay here for the rest of his life. However long that was. On this freezing winter's night, when the only sound to disturb the silence was the distant, repetitive hooting of an owl, Adrian yearned for warmer climes and the hot tropical nights of Kenya, his boyhood home. Instead of owls hooting, he suddenly longed for the sound of rasping cicadas and the short, warm rains that fell from October to December. Anything but this dead, lifeless snow that made him feel as though he were encased in a tomb...

'Can I help you?'

Dropping her basket of laundry in the hall behind her, Liadan pushed some hair out of her eyes, smoothed a hand down her jeans and smiled pleasantly at the smartly dressed blonde who stood on the doorstep.

'I'd like to see Adrian, if I may?'

The woman was clearly about to step inside without being invited, her too-heady perfume was as pushy as she was, and as Liadan's eyes locked on her brittle blue gaze she suddenly recalled Kate's dire warning about reporters trying to inveigle their way in to get interviews with Adrian. Resolved to do everything in her power to prevent any unwanted invasion of her boss's privacy, Liadan quickly stood in front of the woman to block her entrance, her heart missing a beat at this unexpected confrontation.

'Do you have an appointment with Mr Jacobs?'

'He'll see me. My name is Cheryl Kendall. Tell him I've had some new information about his affair with Petra Collins. Tell him I'm going to go ahead and print it unless he gives me an interview.'

Two reactions hit Liadan simultaneously. First, how much she despised the woman's blackmailing tactics, and second, the name Petra Collins. Five years ago she had been one of the hottest properties in Hollywood, a beautiful raven-haired actress with a widely publicised taste for high living and seriously wealthy men. It was well known that since then her career hadn't prospered. Her last film had been three years ago, and that had been a resounding flop at the box office. If the papers were to be believed, the latest news was that she was in some fancy drying-out clinic in California, getting help for her alcoholism. Liadan didn't read the papers much herself but her friends Jennie and Mel were avid consumers of the gossip columns.

'I'll tell him no such thing! Now, please just go. Mr Jacobs is working and he doesn't like to be disturbed when he's—'

'It's okay, Liadan. I'll speak with *Ms* Kendall.'

She spun round in surprise at his voice, and her limbs went strangely weak at the sight of her employer. He was dressed in his usual black; the silver in his hair seemed even more eye-catching against his otherwise sable locks and his eyes were very dark and grave. Weary, almost. The wave of sympathy that rushed through Liadan couldn't be tamped.

'I'll give you five minutes, ten at the most. Come into my study.' His voice curt, Adrian waited briefly for Cheryl Kendall to step inside before striding ahead of her down the corridor.

The stop-start hum of the dryer resounding in her ears, Liadan folded the pile of clothing she had already dried on top of the washing machine, her movements automatic and efficient even as her mind was distracted. Both curious and concerned about the conversation that was going on upstairs right now in Adrian's study, she prayed that Cheryl Kendall's paper or magazine, whatever it was, was not going to print anything injurious or wounding to him. How had Adrian come to meet the famous actress in the first place, and why had their affair ended? Had Petra found him as cold as he appeared? Had she ever managed to get past some of those impenetrable layers that Adrian so obviously protected himself with?

The thought made Liadan stop what she was doing

and stare unseeingly ahead. How had she known that? Adrian Jacobs had been deeply wounded—maybe beyond repair—and now strove to do everything in his power to prevent himself from ever being so badly hurt again. One only had to read his books to know that he was a man who had delved deeply into the realms of his own shadow. You'd have to have spent a lot of time exploring the darker side of the human psyche to come up with some of the twisted and terrifying plots that Adrian came up with in his work. And Liadan's summing-up of what she'd read had been right. There were no redeeming solutions for the human condition in his stories. Not even the merest flicker of light.

'Liadan? Where are you?'

Hearing him call her name, Liadan put her hands up to quell the sudden rush of heat in her cheeks, took a moment to compose herself, then ran up the back stairs into the open hallway to find him waiting for her.

'I'm here. What's wrong?'

For a brief second, Adrian almost forgot what he'd called her for. Again, that gentle perfume reminded him of May blossoms, and the sudden sight of her—all flushed cheeks and big blue eyes and pretty red-gold hair seizing an unexpected chance at liberty from its bun—made him think impossibly of spring. Of hope renewed and life restored after the dead of winter... For a moment the tightening in his throat made it impossible to speak.

'Nothing's wrong. What, did you think I'd be intimidated by some pushy little journo wearing too much make-up with an inflated sense of her own importance? You clearly don't know the newspaper game like I do.'

'Oh.' Feeling the full disturbing force of his gaze, Liadan linked her hands together in front of her, then in the next second unlinked them and folded her arms self-consciously across her chest. Those deep, dark eyes of his were profoundly unsettling. They made Liadan far too aware of her own femininity in a way that no other man had made her feel before. Yet when he glanced away again, clearly too aloof to have stirred such an intimate response, it was as if she'd dreamt the whole thing and her feelings had seriously misled her.

'You're all right, then?'

He grimaced. 'Yes, I'm fine. Come into my study, will you? I need your help.'

The sight that met her on entering Adrian's room had Liadan's blue eyes widening in shock. Practically every inch of floor space was covered in loose pages of manuscript, a chair was upturned and the broken remains of what was once a charming blue and white porcelain coffee cup littered the rug by the piano.

'You can see why I need help,' Adrian said dryly.

'What happened?' Getting down on her knees to recover some of the loose pages, Liadan sensed Adrian start to do the same behind her, the warm, woody drift of his cologne catching her unawares and making her stomach turn hollow.

'My temper happened. People like *Ms* Kendall have a way of bringing out the worst in me.'

'I can see that.' Reaching forward to grab a further wad of papers, Liadan sensed Adrian grow still. 'What's the matter?' Turning her head, she saw a tic in the side of his jaw and his eyes turn dark as molasses.

'Why don't you start on the other side of the room?' he said lightly, the beginnings of a very wry smile tugging at the edges of his usually severe mouth.

'Why?'

'Take it from me, your current position is far too distracting, and I'm only human.'

Feeling her face flame red-hot, to her shame Liadan quickly understood what he meant. She'd been wriggling around on the floor retrieving papers with her bottom stuck up in the air, and with not one notion that Adrian was behind her appreciating the view…

Getting quickly to her feet she beat a swift retreat to the other side of the large room. 'Sorry.'

'Don't apologise, Miss Willow. It's the best thing that's happened to me all day.'

Concluding it was probably wise not to say anything for the next few minutes in case she embarrassed herself even further, Liadan concentrated on the task in hand, her mind racing, wishing she could erase what had just happened and start all over again.

'I have to commend your lack of curiosity, Liadan,' Adrian drawled. 'You didn't ask what Ms Kendall was threatening to print about me and Petra Collins.'

'It's none of my business.' Straightening the pages in her hands, Liadan chose to keep her gaze on the neat, uniform type rather than direct it at Adrian.

'They're threatening to print that Petra was expecting my child—that I made her have an abortion.'

Swallowing hard, Liadan finally looked up. She met Adrian's steady dark gaze without a flinch. 'What do you expect me to say to that?'

'It's a rare woman in my experience who has no curiosity.'

'Your personal business is your business, Mr Jacobs. I'm only your employee.'

'What if I choose to confide in you, Liadan? Would that be too big a burden for those slender shoulders of yours? And by the way…my name is Adrian.'

Feeling heat overwhelm her like the rising steam from water being poured onto hot coals, Liadan lowered the papers to her lap and told herself that she was imagining this whole unbelievable scenario. Why on earth would a man like Adrian Jacobs confide in a woman he had known barely a scant three days when Kate had warned her that he was a closed book, a taciturn loner who wanted the least possible contact with the rest of the human race?

'If you want someone to talk to, then of course I'm willing to listen. You have my word what you say will go no further than this room.'

'I think I already know that, Liadan. That's why I'm going to tell you.'

CHAPTER FOUR

'I WAS introduced to her at dinner at the Dorchester in London by a mutual friend who happens to be a film director.' Straightening to his full height, Adrian paused as if carefully weighing the words he was about to speak. A sudden ferocious gust of wind rattled the windowpane, startling them both with an eerie whistling sound that sent a chill racing down Liadan's spine. On the mantel, the ticking of the clock seemed to grow louder to her suddenly hypersensitive hearing.

Drawing his fingers through his hair almost wearily, Adrian sighed. 'To cut a long story short...we had a fling, a brief sexual liaison that didn't last longer than a couple of weeks. It was stupid of me. I should never have got involved with Petra even for a second. The woman was unstable—irrational. The pressure of superstardom had seriously started to unravel her. We made love, yes, but I took precautions. There was no way that the baby she was supposedly expecting could be mine—if there was ever a baby at all.'

'But someone is saying that there was?'

As if suddenly noticing that she was there, Adrian frowned in surprise as his glance swept over her calm, pretty face. Strangely, it seemed to anchor his thoughts somehow and he felt oddly reassured by her presence.

'Someone?' He laughed harshly. 'Petra's publicity machine, don't you mean? Apparently they seem to think that because my star is on the rise, I could provide a whole lot of free advertising to get Petra Collins' name back in the headlines. That's all this whole far-cical abortion business is about. I never even saw her again after the two weeks we were together were over. She certainly never contacted me to tell me she was pregnant, never mind me ''forcing'' her to have an abortion!'

'They're not going to print those lies, are they?' Liadan spoke in hushed tones, mindful of jarring any further unhappy, unwanted memories.

'Out of the goodness of their hearts they're prepared to buy my side of the story to counter the claims Petra Collins' people want to make public. Damage limitation, they call it.'

'And…have you decided what you're going to do?'

His expression turned suddenly savage. 'I told them to go to hell.'

Her blue eyes taking silent inventory of the mess before her, Liadan concluded that that must have been when he had gone ballistic. And who could blame him? It was sickening that Petra Collins and her publicity machine could dream of slandering Adrian's reputation just to put her back into the spotlight. She secretly hoped that he had put the fear of God into the brittle Cheryl Kendall before she'd left so that the reporter would seriously think twice before darkening his door-step again.

'All I want is to be left alone to work in peace. Why is that so bloody hard?'

Clutching the papers in her hand, Liadan got slowly to her feet. 'Don't let them get to you, Mr Jacobs…Adrian. I believe that people always get their comeuppance. What goes around comes around.'

To her shock Adrian's expression grew even darker, his eyes lost in the pain of some deep inner anguish.

'For God's sake don't tell me that, Liadan! I'm in enough trouble as it is without being reminded that there's always a price to pay for past misdeeds.'

'All of us have skeletons in our closet,' she quickly asserted. 'And I'm no saint. I've got my share of regrets about the past, but I truly believe there's redemption for everyone in the end.'

'Do you?' He was suddenly at her side, his gaze intensely roving her face as if he could somehow extract from her the solution he so desperately seemed to be seeking. Her mouth went dry at his closeness.

'You probably think I'm very naïve to hold such a belief.'

'I have to confess your innocence intrigues me. I do believe that we reap what we sow, but as for redemption?' His hard jaw tightened as if he were struggling to get a purchase on feelings that threatened to drag him under into an abyss that held nothing but terror. 'From who or what? Some imagined force for good that exists in the world to save our souls? I don't think so. Look around you. Even you surely can't avoid noticing that fear and darkness holds most of us in its grip—no matter how hard we might wish things were different.'

Before she could utter another word in her defence, Adrian swung away from her and marched to the door. 'If you could gather up the rest of my papers and put them together into some kind of sane order, I'd be in your debt. I suddenly feel the need for some fresh air.'

It was ridiculous, but Liadan felt devastated that Adrian seemed to believe he didn't deserve to be forgiven for whatever past misdeeds he was overshadowed by. Whatever it was, whatever terrible thing had happened, whatever ghosts he couldn't seem to lay to rest, he surely didn't deserve to be tortured by it for the rest of his life? To shut himself away in this beautiful mausoleum of a house with no contact from anyone but the people who worked for him might help him produce best-selling novels with dark themes that helped fuel people's fears, but was that a good enough reason not to move on with his life and look for something a little more hopeful?

Guiltily shaking herself out of her reverie, she quickly gathered up the rest of the strewn manuscript, stood the upturned chair back in its proper place and painstakingly picked up every shattered piece of broken crockery. Then she spent the next hour collating all the pages of Adrian's script and putting them in a neat, orderly pile on top of his writing desk. Hoping that her efforts might induce him to feel a little calmer on his return, Liadan made to leave the room. Inadvertently glancing at the piano on her way out, she flexed her fingers longingly, then let herself out of the study to return to the utility room and get on with her chores.

'Hello, George. Looks like the snow is finally melting.'

Clapping her hands together briskly in her warm woollen gloves, Liadan let her gaze roam briefly around the large greenhouse, then back again to the head gardener, who was examining seed trays with a frown.

'And everything up to its eyes in muck and bullets,' George replied dourly, before turning to give her his full attention.

'It's pretty while it lasts but I can see why it's not exactly welcome. It can't be easy taking care of gardens this large,' Liadan commented sympathetically.

'It's not normally a problem. Been looking after this

place most of my working life. Took care of these gardens for Mr Jacobs' uncle. I was just a young lad when I started here. You wait till you see them in spring, Miss Willow. You'll see a sight for sore eyes then!'

Feeling a genuine fondness developing for the older man as well as huge respect for his obvious skill and dedication in taking care of the gardens, Liadan let down her guard and started to relax. Whether she would still be here in the spring was another story entirely, but it shouldn't stop her getting to know George a little better. With Adrian locked away in his study most of the time working and more or less on her own in the house, she wouldn't mind someone else to talk to now and then.

'I can't wait. George, I wondered if you had any flowers I could have to put in the house? The place needs cheering up a bit, in my opinion.'

'You asked Mr Jacobs about that, lass?' Frowning, George's light blue eyes were suddenly wary.

'Is there a problem?'

'Mr Jacobs don't usually like flowers in the house, lass. He said they remind him too much of funerals.'

Digesting this new knowledge with a little flutter of disquiet in her chest, Liadan shrugged good-naturedly. 'Nothing's set in stone, though, is it? I just thought a few nice blooms for the drawing room and the hall and maybe a pot of something I could take care of in my room. Hyacinths, perhaps?'

'I'll sort you out something just as soon as I've seen to these trays. Come back in a couple of hours, will you?'

'Thanks, George.'

'You settling in okay up at the house?'

Her smile was as sunny and as soothing as a summer

garden and George found himself unreservedly warming to Adrian's new young housekeeper.

'I'm starting to get used to it. I don't mind saying that I was quite intimidated at first.'

'Don't let Mr Jacobs worry you, lass. His bark is far worse than his bite, I can tell you. Very much like his uncle, he is, and he was a good man too. Never had a cross word from him in my life.'

'Thank you. That's very…reassuring. I'll come back in a couple of hours, then.' As she made her way along the slippery and wet paths that led back to the house Liadan found herself puzzling as to why Adrian would assert that flowers only reminded him of funerals. She got the feeling it had to do with whatever was tormenting him about his past, and her stomach turned over at the thought. Had someone close to him died? Someone he couldn't forget? His wife, maybe?

'Liadan!'

She swivelled at her name, her gaze seeking out who had called her. When she saw Steven Ferrers hurrying towards her, a garden rake hoisted in one hand and his long dark hair flying, she felt every muscle in her body contract warily. What did *he* want?

'I'm glad I caught you.' As he drew near his glance was piercing and far too familiar. Liadan wished she'd got back to the house before he'd seen her, but tried hard to conceal her irritation. George Ferrers was a sweetie but his son was not in the same league as his father. Not by any stretch of the imagination.

'What can I do for you, Mr Ferrers?'

'Oh, come on!' Grinning in disbelief, he swept his gaze down her figure in her long tweed coat and up again to the riot of red-gold curls that the wind had blown free of her bun. 'We don't need to stand on ceremony, do we? My name's Steven. We're both young, both stuck out here in the middle of bloody nowhere, and it's going to be a long winter, sweetheart. What say you and me have a bit of fun? There's a bit of a get-together tonight down at the village hall— some football mates of mine and their girls. I'm sure you could get the evening off if you fluttered those pretty eyelashes of yours at Mr Jacobs.'

The whole idea was so preposterous that Liadan was genuinely astounded. When God had been handing out bare-faced cheek, Steven Ferrers certainly hadn't been lingering at the back of the queue. Flutter her eyelashes at Adrian Jacobs indeed! She could just imagine where that would get her. Then she remembered his dark eyes turning unsettlingly smoky during that incident in his study when he'd asked her to help to pick up his papers. Her heartbeat seemed to quicken and her breath grow suddenly shallow.

'I think I ought to make one thing clear right now, Steven. I'm not looking to have a "bit of fun" with anyone. I'm here to do a job, and that's all. Now, if you'll excuse me, I've got to get back to work.' Liadan was about to turn away, and her blue eyes flew wide in alarm when Steven grabbed her arm none too gently, glaring at her with a hard, almost threatening glance that made her blood run cold. 'Think yourself too good for the likes of me, do you, *angel*? You'll be glad enough of some normal male company after a week working for him up there! He's not interested in women, darling, no matter how pretty. He's got too much ice in his veins for that. You read his books? The only women he's interested in are corpses! Spooky, wouldn't you say?'

Pulling her arm free, Liadan felt as if her bones had

suddenly turned as soggy as wet noodles. The hand she withdrew was visibly shaking in its protective bright orange glove. 'Don't you ever lay so much as a finger on me again, do you hear? If you do I'll speak to the police! I won't even hesitate—*do you hear*?'

It wasn't an idle threat, either. Her friend Mel's father was the local chief constable for the area. The thought comforted her. Alone in this out-of-the-way place, with Adrian too absorbed in his work to have an inkling what was going on should there be some kind of threat, she wanted to make sure that Steven knew she was no easy target for his mischief.

'I thought you looked like a frigid, stuck-up bitch when I first set eyes on you! Your threats don't frighten me, sweetheart. Police, my eye!' As he turned and stamped back up the path towards the greenhouses Liadan let out a long, ragged breath and pressed her gloved hands to the raging heat in her face. She'd sensed that Steven Ferrers would be trouble the moment she'd set eyes on him. She wished her damned intuition had been wrong for once.

Adrian stepped back from the window, unable to suppress the strange sense of betrayal that ebbed through him at the sight of Liadan talking to an animated Steven Ferrers. After he had broken one of his own cardinal rules yesterday and revealed to her information that normally MI5 and the CIA wouldn't be able to drag out of him, Adrian found himself speculating whether he could trust her after all. Young Ferrers was a cocky so-and-so, and definitely not someone to place your trust in. If Liadan didn't have the wits to deduce that for herself, then both of them were in trouble.

Adrian had only employed Steven out of deference

to George; he was well aware of the younger man's employment history. It was unusual if he managed to hold down a job for more than a couple of weeks, according to his records. Clearly allergic to work, he sought out every opportunity to disappear for a smoke and Adrian knew that George had covered for him on numerous occasions when Steven had hopped off home early. Right now he was holding onto his job by a wing and a prayer. That said…what did he want with Liadan? Sighing, Adrian silently answered his own question. Liadan was young, beautiful and available— just by virtue of the fact that she was living and working in Adrian's house. To Steven Ferrers she was doubtless easy pickings.

Irritation growing into disquieting, gnawing rage, Adrian swore and turned back to his computer.

'What are *they* doing in here? I never have flowers in the house…ever! Didn't Kate tell you?'

Her whole body tensing, Liadan turned from dusting the beautiful gold carriage clock on the marble mantelpiece and tried to smile. It was all very well coolly trotting out 'nothing's set in stone, though, is it?' to George Ferrers, but now, faced with what she had done in the light of Adrian's apparent loathing, she couldn't help feeling she'd made a bad decision. Judging by the furious scowl across his deeply compelling features, a *very* bad decision.

'They bring sunshine into the house and light up the room…don't you think?' In the face of his obvious hostility, Liadan's words sounded ineffectual and feeble, like trying to irrigate miles of desert with a watering can. No matter how passionate she was on the subject, she knew she would never convince him that the vivid yellow flowers that filled the beautiful glass vases on either side of the fireplace should stay.

'Get rid of them!' Turning his back, Adrian paused in the doorway, clearly too overwhelmed with anger to even face her. Gazing at the tense stance of those impressively broad shoulders beneath his black cashmere sweater, Liadan concluded it must take a massive amount of mental discipline to contain that much fury and emotion twenty-four hours a day. Didn't he ever get tired of being so angry?

'I'm sorry you don't like them. I'll remove them to my room.'

'What were you doing talking to Steven Ferrers?' Like a whiplash he had spun round to face her again, his dark eyes openly hostile and suspicious.

Because he was confrontational and she was genuinely upset about having to remove the flowers, Liadan raised her chin defiantly.

'Is that against the rules too?'

'When you live under my roof, Liadan, you obey my rules. I'm not interested in whether you like them or not.'

Biting down on her lip, Liadan held onto her own temper by a thread. It didn't matter that she wished Steven Ferrers wouldn't come within ten feet of her, never mind talk to her! What did matter was that she objected to being spoken to like a badly behaved child.

'So what are you saying? That I'm not to converse with the two other members of your staff, ever? That could make things slightly awkward.' Her cornflower blue eyes were glittering, and another emotion besides irritation swept through Adrian as he studied her. Even when she was furious—and he could see that she was—with that tumbling red-gold hair that refused to stay bound and her eye-catching figure in jeans and a white ribbed sweater, she undeniably stirred his blood. Sucking in a deep breath, Adrian strained every muscle in his body to try and tamp down the power of his desire.

'It's Steven I want you to keep away from, as much as possible. George is a good man—you have nothing to fear from him.'

Her heart knocking against her ribs, a vivid image stealing into her mind of Steven Ferrers' face hovering angrily too close to her own—so close that she could smell the tobacco on his breath—Liadan blinked in surprise. 'You're saying I *do* have something to fear where Steven is concerned?'

'Just keep away from him. I don't want him bothering you.' He met her eyes with an intense glance that sent a little zing of heat dancing through her blood, but Liadan told herself she must have imagined the distinct note of concern in Adrian's voice. The only concern he had was to be obeyed to the letter, she thought crossly. Yesterday, when he had confided in her about Petra Collins, now seemed like something she had dreamt—because today he was suddenly a very different man. Today he was definitely the Lord and Master of all he surveyed, and Liadan very much his lowly employee. No doubt he had regretted telling her so much and now sought to establish the proper distance to their relationship, lest she should try and take advantage.

She shouldn't feel so upset at the idea, but strangely she did. She was alone out here, in this big, aloof house, with a man who was about as sociable as a wounded bear and with a growing sense that whatever she did—however perfectly or wonderfully she did her job—it would somehow never be good enough.

'Was there anything else, Mr Jacobs? I really should get on.' Lifting one of the glass vases, Liadan blew a curling red-gold lock of hair from her eyes, striving to keep her gaze as impersonal and unaffected as possible. A frown between his dark brows, Adrian didn't reply straight away. To Liadan's increasing discomfort he seemed to be spending an inordinate amount of time just staring at her. What he was thinking about, she couldn't begin to guess.

'The flowers can stay,' he said gruffly.

Her blue eyes widened in surprise. 'Really?'

'It's not a big deal.'

'Oh, but it is!' Putting the vase back in its place, Liadan straightened, resting her hand momentarily on the marble mantel. 'If putting them here makes you unhappy, I'll take them away to my room. This is your home. You have a right to have things the way you like them.'

Home. Adrian's glance was unremittingly scornful. 'It's people who make a home, Liadan, not bricks and mortar. Take away the people who matter and all you have is a shell. Small or grand—it doesn't matter. It's still a shell.'

Sensing his anguish and frustration, Liadan didn't know what to say. For a moment there she'd never seen anyone look more lost...or more alone.

'Anyway, I'd better put you in the picture about to-morrow.'

'What's happening tomorrow?' Relieved that he'd changed the subject because he would probably only scorn any comfort she tried to offer, Liadan waited with interest for him to tell her.

'Cheryl Kendall's newspaper is printing Petra's claim about the abortion. I fully expect to be invaded in the morning by journalists champing at the bit. My solicitor, Edward Barry, will be here first thing to make a statement on my behalf. Just stay put in the house for a while until they go, will you? I don't want you getting caught up in the free-for-all, and, believe me, it will be one.'

He had that world-weary look in his dark eyes again and this time Liadan really did feel like comforting him. She knew it wasn't her place and that she had no right—she was just someone he'd given a job to, and what did she know of the personal torment he was going through? But she was adamant that he shouldn't have to endure such invasion alone, with nobody on his side but his solicitor.

'Is there anything I can do for you, Adrian?'

'Just do the job I'm paying you to do. There's nothing more you can do for me but that.'

As Adrian turned away from the distinctly hurt look in her lovely blue eyes he wondered when he'd added lying to his list of sins. Right now there was another kind of comfort he'd readily accept from Liadan Willow. And it definitely wasn't a kind that was within the remit of her job. He should put his lustful thoughts about her firmly to the back of his mind and remember that he needed a housekeeper far more than he needed a woman to warm his bed.

Returning to his study, he found it impossible to concentrate on his manuscript. Seeing those bright yellow tulips in the drawing room had foisted a wave of melancholy upon him that he couldn't seem to shake. It wasn't that he hated flowers as such—when everything started to bloom again in the gardens there was nothing he enjoyed more than to walk undisturbed through the meandering paths and admire nature at its most lovely. But flowers in the house reminded him of the cloying, desolate atmosphere of Nicole's home on the day of her funeral. Because it had been raining heavily outside, all the mourners had gathered first at the house and Trevor and Barbara Wilson's home had been full of bouquets and wreaths, the rooms overflowing with them. Their combined sweet cloying scent had almost made Adrian gag.

Now he found that his body was restless and he had a frustration in him that for once wouldn't be beaten into submission by applying himself to work. Dreading the melee and intrusion of newspaper journalists tomorrow, he wished he could escape somewhere where he would never be found again. He'd had a fling with Petra Collins in a weak, despairing moment, fuelled by an excess of alcohol at dinner, and now regretted it bitterly. Adrian could only pray that once this latest nonsense had died a thoroughly deserved death, they would all go away and leave him alone for good.

Knowing he had to divert his restless energy somehow, he put a classical CD in the player, sat in his favourite winged armchair where he could gaze out at the melting snow in a landscape that was usually lush and green, and waited for the music to bring salve to his soul.

Unable to sleep, her mind whirring with thoughts of the morning when a barrage of reporters would apparently be gathering on the front steps, Liadan got out of bed, pulled on her white towelling robe over tartan flannel pyjamas and stepped outside into the long, echoing corridor. Thankfully there was a light still burning and she could see her way down the long, sweeping staircase to the lower floor where the kitchen was. Assuring herself that a glass of hot milk would do the trick and help her to sleep, she opened the door and switched on the light. Her heart almost burst out of her chest in fright when she saw Adrian stare back at her in surprise from the comfort of the kitchen chair he was currently occupying. In his hand he nursed what looked like a glass of scotch. His hooded eyes adjusting themselves to the light, his stern mouth lifted in a mocking little smile.

'Sweet dreams evading you too tonight, Liadan? Perhaps you'd like to join me in drowning my sorrows in a glass of whisky?'

'I'd prefer some hot milk, thank you,' she replied primly, clutching at the tie on her robe to make sure it was secure. Adrian's answering humourless laugh sent goose-bumps flying in all directions across her sensitive skin.

'Of course you would. You probably think there's something sordid about resorting to alcohol in moments of weakness, don't you? Forgive me, Liadan. I don't mean to offend your obviously delicate sensibilities.'

Upset and annoyed by his careless assumptions about her nature, Liadan came fully into the room, facing Adrian with little shooting sparks of fury in her bright blue eyes.

'You should know better than to make such casual judgements about people! You don't like it done to you, so why do you imagine *I* should tolerate it? You think I haven't been so hurt that I can't understand how a person might use a drink or two to try and deaden the pain? Well, think again, Mr Jacobs, because I have.' Biting her lip to stop it from wobbling, Liadan gulped down a deep breath, then walked towards a line of cupboards on the other side of the room, intent on searching out a milk pan to make her drink.

She wouldn't think about Michael right now. Nor would she recall the terrible feelings of deep rejection because when it came down to it she hadn't been able to compete with his faith. But it wasn't just his rejection that had hurt. There were times before he'd made the decision to leave when she had allowed herself to feel less than worthless. Times when he'd berated or scolded her for not being as capable, or intelligent, or faultless as she might be. Times when he'd suggested that her virtue was tainted for ever because she'd slept with a boyfriend when she was twenty and wasn't a virgin. Michael hadn't wanted to sleep with Liadan because she was somehow defiled, unclean in his mind, not just because of his faith.

Behind her she registered the sound of Adrian's chair scraping against the stone-flagged floor. Her spine tensed, as stiff as a steel post.

'Liadan?'

'What?' She found the saucepan and moved away to retrieve a pint of milk from the amply stocked fridge.

'If making assumptions is a fault of mine, I apologise. Here, let me do that.'

'I'm quite capable of—'

'Your abilities aren't in question. I just think you ought to sit down and let me make you a drink. Perhaps this would be a good opportunity for you to tell me a little about yourself. What do you say?'

CHAPTER FIVE

SITTING at the table, her mug of hot milk cradled warmly in her hands, Liadan glanced briefly at Adrian in the chair opposite, trying desperately to come to terms with the strong sensation of intimacy that frighteningly seemed to flow between them.

'What do you want to know?' she asked quietly.

'How long have you lived in the village? It's strange I've never seen you there before.' If he'd seen her he certainly would have remembered her…

'I've been around. I moved here three-and-a-half years ago. Before that I lived in Dorset with my mother. She lives in Spain now.'

'Why didn't you go into the hotel business when you left Dorset? Why did you go to work in an esoteric bookshop, of all places?' He was smiling, but this time not mockingly. Liadan sensed the tension in her stomach ease a little.

'There aren't many hotels in the local vicinity and those I tried didn't have any vacancies at the time. My friend Mel has a friend called Jennie who owned the shop and was looking for someone to help out. As luck would have it, Mel's boyfriend owns the local estate agent's, and he helped me get my mortgage on my cottage when I decided to move here.'

'And this Mel? She lives in the village too?'

'That's why I moved here. We've known each other since we met on holiday when we were kids.' Liadan took a sip of the fragrant creamy milk laced with nutmeg and experienced a rush of surprise that Adrian had made it so perfectly. There was something highly personal about him making it for her—something that very definitely blurred the lines of employer and employee, and made their relationship suddenly far more intimate.

'So…you've been here three and a half years and you're still alone?'

'Alone?'

'No significant other?' Taking a slug of whisky, Adrian made a face as the fiery spirit scorched the back of his throat, then put down his glass and fastened his slow, deliberate gaze on Liadan's face with deepening interest. Her throat convulsed a little, and her grasp on her mug tightened.

'There was someone,' she admitted softly. 'We were going to be married but things between us didn't work out.'

'You decided the married state wasn't for you after all?'

Her heart beating an uneasy tattoo and, unsure of how much to reveal, Liadan shrugged the comment aside and forced herself to continue. 'No. The man I was involved with had a conflict of priorities. It was either me or his calling to the Church. In the end the Church won hands down. I don't blame him. He had a right to follow his heart.'

'And you loved this man?' Adrian's voice sounded like whisky and cigarettes and Liadan found that, as much as she desperately needed to, it was nigh on impossible to break away from the burning intensity in his eyes.

'I… I *thought* I did.' Shrugging her slim shoulders, because there was a wealth of soul-searching behind that statement that she couldn't begin to explain,

Liadan looked pained. It was enough to know that she'd analysed her behaviour deeply and with enough regularity to write a psychology book. 'I don't know if I was actually "in love" with Michael. He was solid and reliable and at the time I thought I needed that.' Until he'd started to dictate what she could or couldn't do, that was.

Feeling as though she had to qualify her statement, particularly what she knew must sound like a complete lack of affection for the man she had been engaged to, Liadan found words spilling from her lips that she hadn't meant to say. 'My father died, you see. I was very insecure after that for a while. He'd appeared so healthy and strong up until his heart attack, and my mother and I had no notion that anything was wrong. It's scary when someone you love suddenly isn't there any more, and we'd always been so close. When he died I was quite lost for a while. Well…for a long time, actually. When Michael came along I suppose he picked that up. In a way he liked the idea of rescuing me, I think. He was very much a man who liked to take charge and he wanted me to defer to him in practically everything—even down to the friends I had. As soon as that started happening I should have known that things would never work out. Anyway…in the end I was relieved he made the decision he did.' She paused, feeling slightly ridiculous for revealing so much, for allowing herself to expose her failings and vulnerability to a man like Adrian who, with his cynicism about the world, probably took it as read that relationships didn't work out—period.

'I wonder if he still believes he made the right choice?' Before Liadan could answer the question, Adrian slid the palm of his hand across her fingers gripping the mug of hot milk, his touch all but scorching her. His skin was smooth and warm and incredibly erotic and for brief seconds such a longing swept over Liadan that she couldn't do anything other than stare deeply into his eyes and let the feeling take her. Her heart slamming against her ribs, she told herself he meant it as a consoling gesture and it was nothing to get worked up about. But somehow her wildly racing heart refused to listen. He must have access to a kind of magic to instil that much magnetism and that much sensation into just one simple brush of his skin against hers, Liadan thought frantically, staring at him in fright.

'I'm sure he does. Why shouldn't he?'

She shot out of her chair, milk slopping out of her mug onto the table, jarred by the suddenness of her movement. Feeling hot colour pour into her cheeks, she swung round in disarray to search for a mopping-up cloth.

'Do you really have to ask why a man wouldn't choose an austere celibate life over being with you, Liadan?' Getting to his feet, Adrian held her gaze for a brief but ignitable couple of seconds before silently locating a dishcloth, wringing it out and mopping up the spill in the middle of the table with quiet efficiency. Watching him, Liadan was mesmerised by the ease with which he moved his fit, muscular body, his movements unconsciously and devastatingly sexy to her hungry eyes, the space he inhabited the compelling focus of her complete and undivided attention.

'Please don't get the idea that sleeping with me was any kind of inducement. As far as Michael was concerned I was…tarnished because I had slept with a boyfriend before.' Looking down at the floor, Liadan wished she didn't still feel humiliated by her ex's judgemental opinion and rejection. 'Besides, I don't think church life is as austere as all that nowadays. At least I hope not. Michael likes his comforts.' She knew she was babbling. She always talked too much when she was nervous and Adrian Jacobs made her very nervous. Lifting her head, Liadan saw that his deliberate dark gaze was examining her with what appeared to be concern in their liquid depths, and she worryingly sensed her equilibrium coming undone. Clutching at the collar of her robe, she tried for a smile but somehow couldn't get the necessary muscles to assist her. 'Thank you for clearing up the spill. I should have done that.'

'So what are you telling me, Liadan? That you and this Michael never actually made love?'

'I think he was waiting for the day when God would personally come down and absolve me of my sins in front of him. He wanted a guarantee that I was good enough.' Her soft mouth twisted with painful humour.

'The man must have been insane.' Adrian shook his head in clear disbelief and Liadan felt a surge of wild gratitude for his vote of confidence.

'I shouldn't have disturbed you,' she said breathlessly. For a long, unsettling moment, Adrian just stared. Then he shook his head as if coming to a decision.

'Go back to bed and get some rest. We both have to be up early.'

Liadan couldn't deny her heartfelt disappointment.

'You were drowning your sorrows and all I did was talk about me.'

'I *asked* you to talk about yourself, remember?'

Adrian wished she would just turn around and leave. In the past few minutes he had become too consumed by the power of her femininity—of all the beguiling attributes that no red-blooded male could fail to notice, starting with her incredible eyes. Her ex-boyfriend either had a will of iron where Liadan's attractions were concerned, or he must have been taking passion-killing drugs to sedate desire, because Adrian couldn't believe that any man could gaze at the woman and not be so turned on that it hurt. And if it was true that a person's eyes reflected their soul, then Liadan's must be as pure and unsullied as water from a crystal well, he surmised with feeling. Because when she trained them on him, all his sins came back with force to haunt him. He was a million miles away from such purity, especially when all he wanted to do right now was tear off her clothes and make violent, passionate love to her.

'What about tomorrow?' she asked tentatively, moving towards the door.

'What about it?'

Aware of his deliberate cooling towards her after the stunning intimacy of the last few moments, Liadan felt her stomach churn with anguish. 'Will you...will you be all right? With the reporters and everything?'

'I'll handle it. Just stay in the house and don't venture out into the gardens unless it's an emergency. After this, I'm going to be installing electronic gates at the end of the drive—something I should have attended to from the beginning. Now go to bed, Liadan. You look tired.'

Deliberately tearing his gaze from the concern in her eyes, Adrian threw the dishcloth into the sink and combed his fingers wearily through his thick dark hair. Instead of soothing him, the whisky he had imbibed had made him irritable and morose—more so now that Liadan was going back to bed. For a few unexpectedly bright moments there she had inspired feelings in him that he'd thought he'd crushed for ever. Feelings of warmth and the need to connect with another human being on a deeper level, not just surface chit-chat that said nothing and concealed everything. Liadan had ignited longings in him that made her a very dangerous woman indeed. A woman who, despite being hurt, still believed in the goodness in the world—who'd forgiven her foolish boyfriend for dumping her because he had a right to 'follow his heart'.

Well, as far as Adrian was concerned, all the goodness in him had long been used up, because he wasn't about to forgive himself for ultimately being the cause of Nicole's death that day. And all because his ego had tricked him into believing he was somehow invincible—immune to threats of death and destruction. It had naturally followed that everyone connected to him had to be invincible too...

Turning her back reluctantly, Liadan told herself that those muscular broad shoulders of Adrian's could handle whatever was troubling him right now. He'd survived this far without any help from her, hadn't he? She just hoped that those reporters tomorrow wouldn't give him too hard a time. Once they had their statement from Adrian's solicitor, she prayed they would just pack up and leave as quickly as possible. She'd make something special for dinner tomorrow night, she decided, her spirits momentarily lifting. A wonderful meal wouldn't solve his problems, but the care she put into preparing it might just convince him that someone cared about his well-being.

'That was a first-rate cup of coffee, Liadan. Thank you. Now, Adrian, my friend, I think we'd better go and appease the wolves, don't you?'

Edward Barry, Adrian's solicitor, surprisingly turned out to be an attractive young man in his mid to late thirties, immaculately dressed in a beautiful Armani suit, his dark blond hair equally impeccably cut and styled. He had a twinkle in his eye that suggested to Liadan that he didn't take himself too seriously, yet at the same time there was a distinct air of reliability about him—as if you could count on him not to let you down. Inwardly Liadan was hugely relieved. Adrian needed someone like Edward Barry on his side right now. The crush of reporters at the door was truly frightening to her inexperienced eye and she couldn't wait for them to be gone. They'd been camping out in the gardens of the house since before dawn with their cars and their camera equipment, apparently immune to the now-slushy melting snow and the biting cold, clearly willing to endure any hardship in anticipation of coming face to face with their quarry.

Bending forward to clear the table of drained cups and saucers, Liadan briefly caught Adrian's eye. It was hard to detect exactly what was going through his mind just then because his attractive face was carefully blank. She wanted to say 'good luck' or something like that but decided that it sounded too asinine. Like wishing someone good luck when they were about to be thrown to the lions, she silently reflected. So instead she just ventured a smile, hoping he knew that she prayed his encounter with the press wouldn't be too awful or painful.

Adrian's arresting dark eyes narrowed briefly, as if silently acknowledging her support, then without further preamble he opened the door and led his solicitor out of the kitchen.

Making herself return to the rooms on the second

floor that needed vacuuming, Liadan headed straight for one of the two large windows in the first room that overlooked the front gardens, unable to resist taking a peek outside. The stone steps were covered in wall-to-wall people, all, it seemed, shouting Adrian's name, demanding he look this way or that while cameras popped aggressively. Like a swarm of vultures fighting over a carcass. Her pulse racing, Liadan bit down on her thumb, the force of her teeth almost biting through the flesh. Anger, swift and powerful, roared through her blood at the sight that met her gaze. How dared they? How dared they invade his home like this, as if they had every right to storm in like some self-righteous marauding army? Surely they must know this whole sorry episode had been engineered by Petra Collins' publicity machine, purely to make her look good and Adrian look bad?

Not even concerning herself with why she so readily believed Adrian's side of the story, Liadan raised her hand to the window, letting her palm rest against the icy glass pane. Her ears strained to hear above the noise as Edward Barry's impressive voice begged for quiet so that he could make a statement on Adrian's behalf.

At the end of the statement, which was dignified yet blunt, and in no way stooped to denigrate Petra Collins either as a woman or as an actress, Edward led Adrian back inside and the crowd on the steps reluctantly started to disperse. Moving away from the window with a sigh, relieved that Adrian's ordeal was for the moment at an end, Liadan switched on the vacuum cleaner to resume her work.

But as the harsh sound filled the formerly silent room she forced herself to remember that she was after all only Adrian Jacobs' housekeeper and not even some-

one he might think of as a friend. She had no need and
no right to concern herself unnecessarily about his welfare. But even though logic begged her to see sense,
Liadan couldn't prevent the helpless yearning that
seemed to have taken root in her heart since their impromptu conversation in the kitchen last night. All she
could do was pray that she would snap out of such
foolishness soon…

At lunchtime she took Adrian coffee and sandwiches. As she rested the tray on top of the piano as
usual Liadan glanced at him sidelong to try and gauge
his mood. They hadn't exchanged words since Edward
Barry had left earlier, because Adrian had gone directly
back to his study to work. Now as she watched him,
his attention apparently wholly absorbed by what was
on the computer screen in front of him, she marvelled
at the fact that he could lose himself in his work so
thoroughly when this morning he'd had to face that
horrible unsettling scene on his doorstep.

'How's it going?' Liadan surprised herself with the
question. She hadn't intended to ask it and, now that
she had, she wished she hadn't. Adrian turned his head
to stare at her as if only just realising she was there.

'Okay.' He didn't elaborate and Liadan knew it was
probably a hint that she should not disturb him any
further and leave. But somehow, because she had been
so concerned about him, she couldn't just leave things
at that without satisfying herself that he really was
okay. 'No man is an island,' the phrase went, and right
now she surmised he could probably use a friend or
two.

'What's the book about?'

As he shook his head slightly Adrian's dark gaze
became immediately guarded—as if he'd endured

enough invasion into his privacy for one day and wouldn't endure any more.

'Why do you want to know?'

'I'm interested.'

Folding her arms across her sky-blue sweater, Liadan smiled. *Brave it out,* she told herself. Don't let him frighten you off with those foreboding dark glances of his.

'You don't like my books. There are no happy endings, remember? Only the inevitable conclusion that life is dark and ultimately dangerous and we'd better arm ourselves in any way we can to deal with it.'

'That's a very sad and pessimistic outlook, if you don't mind my saying.'

Adrian shrugged. 'You can say what you like. It's the truth.'

'No, it isn't.' Her passionate conviction that he was so wrong prevented Liadan from being more cautious. Feeling heat rush into her face, she forced herself to meet his suddenly hard, unflinching glance.

'Life is what you make it. The old saying is true. If you believe everything is dark and dangerous and you should be prepared to meet the worst, then that's what you'll probably pull towards you. But if you nurture optimism and expect the best—then that's what you'll attract. I know you must have been hurt in the past and you've seen some things in your career that no one should ever have to witness, but you shouldn't let it colour your future. *Whatever* happened.'

Pain cramped his throat as old, hurtful memories suddenly deluged him—in particular Nicole lying on that hard sun-baked sidewalk, her beautiful hair caked in blood... Adrian got up from his chair and paced angrily to the window. Just who the hell did this

woman think she was, walking in here and telling him
he shouldn't let his past colour his future? She hadn't
even lived yet!

'Do me a favour, will you? Keep your cosy little
homilies about life to yourself, Liadan. I hired you to
be my housekeeper—not my life coach. If I feel the
need to converse with someone like that I'll go and see
a professional. Understood?'

Staring at his coldly handsome face as he glared
back at her, Liadan tried bravely to field the hurt and
embarrassment that washed over her. She'd only been
trying to help—not fix his life. Did he really think she
had the audacity to do that? She knew her own limi-
tations. Her own life was hardly perfect. Yet, no matter
what happened, she knew what she'd said was true.
Life *was* what you made it...

'I'm sorry you feel that way. I meant no offence, I
was only trying to help.'

'The best way you can help me is to remember what
I hired you for. Do that and we'll get along just fine.'

Having been put firmly in her place and knowing it
was useless to say another word, Liadan nodded
briefly, then turned and walked away. Just as her hand
pushed at one of the double doors to open it she remembered something she'd been going to ask earlier
but had forgotten. In the light of what had just transpired, the question seemed even more imperative.

'I've got to go into the village this afternoon for
some groceries. Would you mind if I took an extra half
hour just to pop back to my cottage to check on
things?'

'No. That's fine.'

'Thank you.'

'Liadan?'

'What?' Her back stiffening, she steeled herself against another admonition.

'If you come across any reporters lurking about or trying to hassle you in any way, come straight back here, do you understand? Forget the groceries until to-morrow.'

'I can deal with—'

'No. You can't. You have no idea what these people can be like. Just do as I say, will you?'

Emotion threatening to overwhelm her, Liadan bit her lip and nodded reluctantly. It would be a big mis-take to imagine for even one second that he was con-cerned for her welfare. He was only trying to protect himself by suggesting she didn't talk to reporters. Did he think she would tell them anything? Sad that there was obviously such a lack of trust, she hurried back down the corridor to the kitchen, suddenly desperate to be out in the fresh air and on her way to the village.

As soon as Liadan arrived at the cottage Jack Kempsey, her lovely elderly neighbour, came round with Izzy, the petulant long-haired Persian she had acquired from the Cats Protection League. As Liadan sank gratefully onto her overstuffed couch with its startling array of vividly bright cushions, her gaze drinking in the cosy front room that she had so missed these past few days, she cradled Izzy on her lap, her fingers stroking the silky fur with unashamed enjoyment.

'I didn't expect to see you so soon.' Jack smiled. 'Got time for a cup of tea before you go back, love?'

'Oh, Jack, you're a godsend! Yes, please. How has Izzy been behaving herself?'

'You don't need to worry about her, Liadan. She's been spoiled rotten, she has! Comes over to me during the day to be fed and acts like the Queen of Sheba, then at night she comes back home through the cat-flap and acts like she's guarding the place for you until you get back.'

'That's my girl.' Tickling the contentedly purring feline beneath her chin, Liadan felt herself shrug off the tension of the morning. Coming home, even briefly, anchored her somehow, reminded her that if things didn't work out up at the big house, then she still had a home to return to. No matter what happened, what kind of work she had to do, she would do it to keep this little house. It was her haven. 'Drowsy Haunt', it was named, and as soon as Liadan was back within its four walls all her cares and concerns seemed to melt away.

'How are you finding it working up there with the writer fellow?' Jack called from the kitchen.

On a scale from one to ten? Below zero... Liadan reflected silently. Then she pulled herself up short, re-minding herself that it wasn't all bad. It was a beautiful house to work in, the work was, on the whole, second nature, and Adrian Jacobs...could be worse. She let loose a wry laugh at that.

'What did you say, love? I didn't hear you.' Popping his head round the door, Jack's wrinkled brow creased in puzzlement.

'I said it's fine, Jack. Everything's fine.'

'Good. It does my heart good to see you smile again. When you were with that Michael fellow, I missed your smile.'

For the umpteenth time that afternoon Adrian glanced at his watch and for the umpteenth time was unable to suppress the sense of worry and anxiety that surged into his chest. *Where was she?* She'd been gone too long even if she had popped back home to her cottage. The perfectly made chicken sandwiches she'd brought him earlier lay curled up and uneaten on the plate and his coffee too had been left to grow cold and congeal in its brightly patterned cup and saucer. After the events of this morning and that scene with Liadan before she'd left to go to the village, the last thing Adrian could stomach was food. The darkly dramatic themes of his current work in progress, instead of exciting or enthusing him, just filled him with melancholy and a silent rage at the futility of his life that was growing daily. Why couldn't he have been the one who'd been left waiting on the sidewalk when the bomb had gone off? Why had it had to be Nicole—vibrant, beautiful and only twenty-nine? She would have been his wife…the mother of his children.

Stalking restlessly from his study, Adrian headed to the kitchen and prowled there, noting the spotlessly clean worktops, meticulously swept floor and newly laundered tea towels folded neatly over the rail of the Aga—all signs that Liadan was completely professional and adept at doing her job. The job he'd hired her to do. He should feel gratified, he told himself. When he'd first seen her he'd doubted she would last a day, never mind impress him with her efficiency. And now he would do well to remember that she was only his housekeeper, not someone he could get close to, whom he might confide in—no matter how beguiling that gentle voice or how kind that beautiful face.

Tapping his fingers against the tabletop, Adrian couldn't resist another glance down at his watch. Where the hell was she? She'd left the house over three hours ago and it was now black as tar outside. Had she been waylaid by the press and somehow persuaded to talk? Or had she simply decided to leave and not come back? Hating the idea and despising himself for dreading such a possibility, he went in search of his coat and, with a surge of energy that had so far been denied him that day, decided to find Liadan and bring her safely back home.

CHAPTER SIX

WHEN he came upon the old-fashioned Morris Minor tilted sideways into a ditch at the side of a winding unmade road not far from the house, Adrian knew immediately it was Liadan's. Climbing quickly out of his Jeep, he ran to the vehicle, his heart pounding so heavily in his chest that it made the blood roar in his ears. As he wrenched open the passenger door and called her name she turned and stared at him, her blue eyes dazed yet startled. Then he saw the blood.

For one terrible, frozen moment Adrian felt physically sick. The blood had oozed from a gash high on her forehead into her beautiful red-gold hair and her skin was quite pale in the car, reflected light from the still blazing headlamps lighting up the interior with an almost supernatural glow.

'I hit my head, I think.' Her smile was lopsided and apologetic. Long training forcing him to take charge even though his heart was still banging like a drum, Adrian leaned towards her in a brisk, no-nonsense kind of way that belied the turmoil going on inside him.

'I need to get you out of there and take you straight to Casualty. Here, reach over to me carefully. Take your time, don't rush.'

She was a warm bundle of tweed coat, bright orange scarf and tumbling strawberry-blonde hair in his arms and if he was surprised at the feeling of protectiveness that washed over him, Adrian quickly squashed the sensation in order to do what he had to do.

'I swerved to avoid a rabbit.' Biting her lip, Liadan stared up at him, tears washing those perfectly blue eyes like a crystal fountain flowing over sapphires.

'A rabbit?' Adrian's expression was almost painfully wry as he eased her gently into the passenger seat of the Jeep. Swiftly fastening her seat belt, he pushed back her hair from her eyes to examine the wound she'd sustained. The gash was about two inches long and appeared deep. He frowned into her upturned face, torn with the need to either scold her thoroughly or kiss her senseless. Again his feelings stole a march on him and he fought hard to get them under control, inwardly raging that right now *nothing* in his life yielded to his control. Not one damn thing, it seemed.

'Here.' He produced a spotless white handkerchief from his jeans pocket and gave it to Liadan. 'Hold this to your head until we get to the hospital. It's about ten miles away. Think you'll be okay?'

'I'll be fine.' Her voice was raspy with a slight catch in it and Adrian's dark gaze grew even more concerned.

'Are you hurting?' he demanded. 'Feeling dizzy or sick?'

'I'm not dizzy but it—it stings.' Wincing, Liadan gingerly pressed the clean white handkerchief to her head. 'You probably think I'm a terrible driver, don't you? But I really thought I'd kill that rabbit.'

'And what if you had killed yourself, huh? Did you think of that when you were trying to do your good deed for the day?'

He sounded furious, Liadan thought a little desperately as her head throbbed. It was fortunate that Adrian had come along when he had because God knew how long she would have been stranded there in rapidly deteriorating freezing temperatures if he hadn't—but *why* did it have to be him who found her in such vulnerable circumstances? She tried to swallow but the ache in her throat was almost as painful as the gash she had sustained.

'I didn't think about trying to do a ''good deed''. I acted completely instinctively. Would *you* like the death of an innocent creature on your conscience?' She knew she sounded petulant but she couldn't help herself. Why did he always have to be so *angry* with her?

Staring at her as if she'd slapped him, his mouth a foreboding grim line in his suddenly pale face, Adrian nodded at her briefly before slamming the door shut at her side. Jumping into the driver's seat, he started the engine, engaged the gears and drove off past Liadan's stranded car without so much as a backward glance, her unfortunately significant words echoing through his brain like the sound of a blacksmith's hammer coming down hard on an anvil. *Would you like the death of an innocent creature on your conscience?* she'd asked. He'd felt so bloody desolate just then that if Liadan hadn't been his passenger, Adrian would have willingly driven his own car into a ditch. Or failing a ditch, the nearest river...

When the door opened suddenly and Adrian strode into her room, Liadan pushed herself guiltily up into a sitting position against the plumped up pillows on the bed, trying to ignore the renewed stinging of her newly stitched wound. They'd spent nearly three hours at the hospital waiting for her to be seen and her wound attended to, and by the time they'd got home it had been nearly ten in the evening. She hadn't been able to even think about cooking him the delicious meal she'd intended, and she guessed her recently bought ingredients were still in the back seat of her stranded car.

Her brows knitting anxiously together, she glanced up at Adrian's tall, imperious figure with a little knot of trepidation settling uncomfortably beneath her ribs. He'd been faultlessly attentive and solicitous at the hospital, regularly checking that she was comfortable enough as they waited on hard red plastic chairs in the busy emergency department. Every now and then he'd stride across the shiny floor to the little reception window and enquire how much longer it would be before Liadan was attended to. All eyes had been drawn to him. He was an imposing-looking man at the best of times and he was even more so when he took charge on Liadan's behalf. She didn't know whether she'd been seen more quickly than she would otherwise have been because Adrian had simply worn the receptionist down with his constant badgering, or because he had the kind of aura about him that plainly commanded attention. In any case Liadan had been grateful to have him on her side.

Now, though, she couldn't help fretting that he must think her a complete nuisance. He needed a house-keeper, not a patient. Knowing that thought must be uppermost in his mind, Liadan resolved to get straight back to her chores in the morning, throbbing head or no throbbing head. She was determined to let Adrian know she was no wilting flower, fading at the first little setback.

'How are you feeling?' he asked, examining her closely.

'Fine.' She gulped, then quickly glanced away lest he see she was lying, because she didn't feel fine. She felt bloody awful if he wanted to know the truth.

'Liar,' he said.

Liadan sensed that uncomfortable knot beneath her ribs tighten. Lifting her hand cautiously to the white gauze dressing that was taped to her forehead, she forced a smile. 'Obviously I've felt better. But it's only a small gash and tomorrow I'll be up and about again, no worries. You'll see.'

'Over my dead body.' Adrian's expression was darkly foreboding. Her eyes widening in surprise, Liadan's heart skittered.

'What do you mean?'

'I mean only an idiot would consider getting up and carrying on as normal after an accident. You need at least a day to recover, if not two. And you're to tell me right away if you have any dizziness or sickness, is that clear?'

Wishing he wouldn't look quite so formidable, Liadan felt herself slump resignedly back against the pillows. All of a sudden she was deathly tired. 'I'll see how I feel in the morning,' she said quietly.

Studying her pale complexion along with the soft, bruising smudges beneath her startlingly blue eyes, Adrian reached out his hand and lifted a curling lock of her red-gold hair. Staring at it, twining it round his fingers, its silken texture stirring something deep within his soul, he frowned, his concentrated dark gaze not moving from the sight of it. It had been shocking when he'd seen the blood staining that beautiful hair. For a moment he really hadn't known where he was, as all the harshly buried pain he'd carried around with him in the years following Nicole's brutal death had seemed suddenly to surface and threaten to batter him—like volcanic rocks spewing down a mountainside towards him. Thank God he'd come quickly to his senses and got Liadan to the hospital as rapidly as he had. He'd never have been able to forgive himself if he hadn't come to her aid in time.

'Head wounds can be very serious—even if they don't appear so at the time,' he said out loud.

He was far away from her in another place, Liadan realised, his mind clearly dwelling on some past situation that she was excluded from. Whatever it was, it haunted him. Haunted him to his very bones. One day when she was brave enough, perhaps she would dare to ask him about it? But not now, when the memory was clearly paining him anew, and especially not when her heart was pumping so hard she almost couldn't breathe…

'I'll be… I'll be careful,' she promised, her lips trembling a little.

'I've called out the chap who owns the local garage to come and get your car out of the ditch. I'm just waiting to hear back from him. As soon as he locates it I'll drive out to talk with him. Will you be all right if I'm gone a little while? I'll be back as soon as I can.'

'I'm sure I'll be just fine.'

'You're not to get out of bed or move so much as a muscle.'

'I won't.'

'Good.' Seemingly satisfied, Adrian abruptly released the impossibly soft coil of hair still brushing against his fingers and strode across the room to the door.

'It's very good of you to do all this. I mean, seeing to my car and taking me to the hospital and everything. I'm very grateful.'

'Don't be.' With a flash of barbed humour, Adrian

shrugged carelessly. 'I'm only protecting my invest-
ment.'

Crushed, Liadan shut her eyes, warding off the hurt
that ached right down to her fingertips.

She was making soup for their lunch. She'd had to
swear by all that was holy to Adrian that she wouldn't
overdo it, but he had finally relented and let her come
downstairs. All the ingredients she needed were laid
out carefully on the scrubbed pine table. Chopped-up
celery stalks filled a blue ceramic bowl next to a dish
of roughly sliced carrots and next to that was a smaller
dish of finely diced onion and garlic. Having spent
years helping in the kitchen of her parents' hotel,
Liadan favoured an ordered approach to her cooking.
Once all her ingredients were prepared and on display,
then she could get down to the fun part of creating
appetising meals. Now as she stood at the stove stirring
a large pan of simmering stock she breathed in the
fragrant cooking smells and tried not to concentrate on
the dull, aching throb in her forehead.

Adrian had warned her not to get carried away. A
sandwich and a cup of coffee would suffice for lunch,
he'd told her as his dark serious gaze had swept brood-
ingly across her features. But Liadan surmised the man
needed to get a bit more creative, at least as far as his
lunchtime routine went. And there was nothing better
than hot, home-made soup on a bright, cold winter's
day like today.

'Anybody home?'

Liadan turned at the voice, and her gaze collided
dazedly with a smiling Steven Ferrers. He strolled into
the big country kitchen with his usual bad-boy stride,
his too-intrusive glance flicking up and down her

sweater-and-jeans-clad figure, making it obvious that he liked what he saw. Liadan's hackles rose immediately, just as Izzy's did when unfamiliar visitors came into the house.

'What are you doing in here? How did you get in?'

She hadn't seen him since that unpleasant encounter in the garden and she was seriously bothered by the fact that he didn't seem to have paid any attention to what she'd said to him then about keeping away from her.

'That's a nice greeting, I must say! Front door was open, for your information. Our Mr Jacobs has gone for a walk and left it ajar. I only dropped by to see how you were. Dad told me you drove your car into a ditch last night and his lordship had to take you to hospital. You've hurt your head. I'm sorry to see that, Liadan.'

Unsure how to handle Steven's professed concern about her welfare and slightly discomfited by the fact that Adrian wasn't present in the house, Liadan wasn't about to let her guard down just yet.

'It's not as bad as it looks. I'm perfectly fine, actually.'

'I won't argue with that, sweetheart. You're easily the best thing in this whole godforsaken place!'

'Look.' Exasperation getting the better of her, Liadan folded her arms across her chest and sighed. 'I really must get on. I've got work to do and I'm sure you have, too.'

'Seen the papers this morning?'

Before Liadan could answer one way or the other, Steven drew a folded-up newspaper from one of the deep patch pockets on his duffel coat and slapped it on the table in front of her.

'Look on page two and cast your eyes over what our infamous Mr Jacobs has been up to!'

When Liadan deliberately made no move towards the offending tabloid newspaper and instead stared frostily at Steven, he leant forward and opened the pages himself for her to examine. Reluctantly Liadan's gaze fell on the grainy black and white picture of Adrian, clearly taken in his days as a war correspondent. He was standing in some kind of desert landscape and he wore light-coloured trousers with the sleeves of his shirt rolled up to the elbows. Even though he must have been reporting from some dangerous and grim terrain, he looked much less careworn and younger than he did today—as if he could easily deal with whatever trials life threw his way and still have reserves left over.

Her stomach clenched tight as though there were suddenly a giant-sized knot inside it. Next to the picture of Adrian there was another more glamorous snapshot of a beautiful brunette with exotic slanting eyes and pouting lips. Petra Collins. The headline screamed, HOLLYWOOD ACTRESS CLAIMS WRITER LOVER DEMANDED ABORTION. Casting her eye further down the page, Liadan briefly read, 'Well-known author Alexander Jacobsen—previously war correspondent Adrian Jacobs—denies Petra Collins' startling claim that he made her have an abortion when she was pregnant with his child...'

'This is garbage.' Grimacing with distaste, she closed the paper and turned back to stir the fragrant-smelling stock in the pan.

'Know that for sure, do you, sweetheart?'

To her alarm, Steven came up behind her and laid his hand on her shoulder. His touch made Liadan shud-

der as though a bug had just crawled down her bare
skin and she swung round and pushed her hands
roughly against his chest to make him go away. 'I told
you before, if you ever lay your hands on me again I'll
call the police!'

'Think your threats can scare me, little Miss Goody
Two Shoes? Just who the hell do you think you're sav-
ing yourself for—the Lord of the Manor? He might bed
you, sweetheart, but don't expect any more than that.
You've seen what he did to that actress. When he mar-
ries it won't be to the likes of you or her. It'll be to
some posh tart that went to the right school whose
daddy is loaded. You could do worse than be nice to
me, Liadan. A *lot* worse.'

His mouth was twisting cruelly, and the macabre
grin made her blood run cold. Trembling with emotion,
Liadan shook her head. 'If you want to delude yourself,
fine! Enjoy your little daydream while it lasts, because
if you so much as come within ten feet of me again
I'll go straight to your father and tell him exactly what
you've been doing.'

'No, you won't.'

'Yes, I w—'

'What's going on here?' Adrian stepped inside the
room with a face like a thundercloud. Liadan's heart
almost stopped. Grabbing up the paper from the table,
she quickly folded it and shoved it into Steven's hands.
The last thing Adrian needed to see today was that vile
slander.

'Nothing.' She smiled, her blue eyes silently signal-
ling Steven to keep quiet. With another self-satisfied
grimace, the younger man touched the paper to his
head as though doffing his cap and sauntered past
Adrian as though he didn't have a care in the world.

'Just a minute.'

'Yes, Mr Jacobs?'

'I don't want you coming in here bothering Liadan when she's working. Is that understood?' Although Adrian's smooth, even voice belied it, Liadan could hear the rage that simmered beneath the calm surface when he addressed the younger man.

'Yes, Mr Jacobs.'

'And you'd better take that stupid smirk off your face right now before I take it off for you!'

'Is that a threat?'

'If you want to keep your job you'd better not even think about getting cute with me. Do I make myself clear, *Mr* Ferrers?'

Clearly struggling to keep a lid on his temper, Steven nodded his head derisively before stalking from the room looking as if he was going to kick the nearest thing that came into contact with his boot.

Letting go of the breath she'd been holding, Liadan pressed her hand to her chest, her fingers closing over a tiny pearl button on the roll-neck collar of her soft wool sweater.

'You should know better than to encourage him.' Arms akimbo, Adrian studied her as if she was a great disappointment to him. Indignation and hurt welled in Liadan's chest at his careless assumption about her association with the younger man. Did he really think she'd be interested in a low-life like Steven Ferrers?

'I didn't! I mean I don't! He just wanted to—'

'I'm not interested in what he wanted from you, Liadan. Things would run a lot more smoothly round here if the people I employed just got on with their jobs and kept the organisation of their social lives for their days off!'

As he strode out of the room Liadan took a moment
to absorb the outrageous admonition before haring off
after him and catching up to him in the corridor.
Unable to think past the fury that was threatening to
burst out of her like a hot spring, she caught his arm
to make him stop and face her.

Adrian stared down at the pale, slender fingers
curved round his bicep, and couldn't deny the fierce
stab of heat that went straight from his arm to his groin.
For a moment it made him almost dizzy—weak with
longing. With her blue eyes flashing and her chest
heaving, right now Liadan Willow was the woman of
his dreams, the epitome of all his fantasies rolled into
one gorgeous, sexy package…

'Just a minute! You can't just walk in, say something
as insulting as that and then walk out again!'

'You don't think I have a right to admonish you if
you waste your time making social arrangements with
Steven Ferrers when I'm paying you both to work for
me?'

Suddenly aware of exactly where her hand was resting, Liadan snatched it back, her pale face awash with
burning heat. All she could think of was one thing now
she had felt the throb of that steely bicep beneath her
fingers…*sex*. Adrian Jacobs was sex on legs and just
lately it had been slow, sweet torture to even be in the
same room as him. Never in all her twenty-seven years
had Liadan experienced such wanton longing for a
man.

'I don't even like the man! Why do you think I
would even dream of seeing him after work?'

'It's not such a stretch of the imagination, is it? He's
not bad-looking, I suppose, and he certainly has a reputation for being a bit of a magnet for some of the

local girls, so I'm told.' Adrian shrugged and glanced away. When he next rested his dark brown eyes on Liadan, one corner of his usually stern mouth had disconcertingly lifted in a little half-smile. 'Maybe you're lonely? You're a young, healthy woman, Liadan—barring head wounds caused by an aversion to running over rabbits. I'm sure you have the normal desires of any young female. You don't have to be ashamed of them.'

Barely able to speak over the dryness in her mouth, Liadan frowned. 'I'm not ashamed. I'm just not interested in Steven Ferrers and I don't want you believing that I am.'

'Good.' His voice arrestingly low, Adrian brushed back a curl from her forehead and seemed to be examining the gauze pad that was still taped there. His touch immediately sent tiny electrical currents of shock pulsing throughout Liadan's body. She felt shivery with heat, weak with fervent, helpless longing, as if her insides were slowly but inexorably melting.

'I like this sweater,' he said beguilingly, his hand moving away from her forehead and resting instead on the front of her mulberry-coloured jumper.

'Do you?' Mesmerised by his hot glance, Liadan hardly dared breathe.

'It shows off your shape to perfection.'

She sensed his fingers move inevitably downwards until they stroked across the burgeoning nub of her nipple, peaked inside her pretty lace bra. Her womb contracted deeply in shock, and a violent wave of scalding desire throbbed through her body leaving her momentarily dazed.

'Adrian, I—'

He withdrew his hand, but his glance still burned.

Liadan could feel the prickling sensation on her breast where he had touched her, the primitive aching need between her legs...

'Keep away from Steven Ferrers. Take it from me, he's trouble. If he bothers you in any way I want you to tell me right away. Understand?'

All she could do was nod. Right now she was hardly capable of speech.

'Oh, and Liadan?'

'What?'

'If you could take pity on me and not wear that tight sweater again, I'd be very much obliged.'

With her face flaming a vibrant scarlet, Liadan turned without a word and hurried back to the kitchen.

CHAPTER SEVEN

'LEAVE that. I think you've done enough for one day, don't you?'

'I'm only setting the table for your dinner. It won't take a minute. I haven't made anything fancy tonight—just a lasagne with a salad.'

Flushing a little, because seeing him again had reminded her that he had all but reduced her to a puddle on the floor with that electrifying brush of his fingers across her breast, as well as his comment about her sweater, Liadan continued to lay the table. At lunchtime she had taken him soup and sandwiches, leaving the tray as usual on top of the beautiful grand piano that she itched to play. Apart from a polite inquiry about her head, he'd let her appearance pass without comment, his work commanding his attention again almost immediately. Liadan had been glad to leave him to eat his lunch in peace and return to the kitchen to eat hers.

But now Adrian wasn't absorbed by work. Dressed in casual black jeans and a chocolate-brown sweater that highlighted his exceptional physique in a way that made Liadan a little more than hot under the collar, he smiled at her as he came into the room, his face looking less careworn than it had in days. That smile had her spirits soaring as high as a bird and she was fiercely glad that she had prevented him from seeing that despicable rag masquerading as a newspaper that Steven had shoved under her nose earlier.

'Why don't you join me?'

'You mean, eat in here with you?'

'Would it be such a hardship, Liadan?'

'No.' Liadan frowned as she straightened up from the table. 'It wouldn't be a hardship at all. That wasn't what I meant. It's just that—'

Looking amused, Adrian casually rubbed his hand round the back of his neck. 'It's just that what?'

Did he really have to ask? Liadan wondered in exasperation. He'd already emphasised more than once that he was paying her to do a job for him, nothing more. Sitting down in his grand dining room to eat dinner with him would be too awkward for words. It would make it hard for her to remember that she was just his housekeeper and not something far more intimate, and to Liadan's mind it was best if she kept the distinction between their roles clear. At the end of the day, Adrian was her employer and she his employee. She needed to hold onto this job if she was going to keep her little house and that had to be her priority. Not some pie-in-the-sky hope that her relationship with her employer might become more personal.

'It would be better if I just ate in the kitchen as normal. You should relax and unwind after your day's work. Dinner won't be long.'

She accidentally came into contact with his arm as she brushed past him to get to the door, and almost leapt out of her skin when Adrian caught her by the wrist to waylay her.

'What if I'm in the mood for some conversation?' he asked idly, his deep, penetrating gaze drifting over her features. Even with that stark white dressing peering out from under her unruly curls, her face was bewitching, Adrian thought hotly. Her pretty mouth had

a naturally gorgeous pout to it and her cute retroussé
nose was probably the envy of all her friends. But when
it came to her eyes, those long-lashed sapphire-blue
orbs that excited him with the merest glance... Well,
if he were a poet instead of a fiction writer, he'd write
poems to her beauty till the day he died. Feeling the
fragile bones of her wrist beneath his fingers, he tightened his hold a fraction longer than necessary before
letting go, just to remind himself what touching her
could do to his already-heightened senses.

'Did Kate ever join you for dinner?' Her voice
sounded a little breathless and with an undeniable throb
of pleasure Adrian knew that his touch had been the
cause.

'No. She was a busy little body who liked to get on
with her work so I never asked her.'

'So you would have...asked her, I mean, if she'd
been predisposed?'

'Suddenly I'm in uncharted waters, Liadan. What exactly are you getting at?'

'I'm your housekeeper, Adrian, not your dinner
guest. It's best we keep things clear, don't you think?'

For a moment his expression was as implacable as
iron. Then in the next second his facial muscles seemed
to visibly relax and he issued her with a brief but
slightly weary smile. 'You're right, of course. Thank
you for the timely reminder.'

Knowing that she had been the cause of his sudden
return to formality and realising it was probably too
late to rescind, Liadan reluctantly left him alone to go
and see to the dinner. But as she returned to the kitchen
she was unable to easily dismiss the powerful longing
that stirred inside her—even when she crossly told herself it was utterly and irrevocably futile.

*   *   *

Later that evening, long after Liadan had gone to bed, Adrian pulled out a single drawer in his writing desk and extracted the slim black volume that lay there. Flicking through its thickly embossed pages, he frowned down at an address and telephone number that he'd inscribed there long ago. His mind made up on what he was going to do, he picked up the telephone and started to dial.

The sun streaming into her room was too bright, like an upturned can of daffodil-yellow paint exploding onto a cream carpet. It was an assault on the senses— an abomination. Her head throbbing, Liadan groaned, got out of bed on legs that felt like rubber and irritably closed the offending gap between the curtains.

'Liadan! Are you in there?'

A loud rapping on the door followed Adrian's harshly raised voice making Liadan freeze where she stood as realisation dawned. What on earth did she think she was doing, going back to bed? It was seven-thirty in the morning, her clock said so, and she should have been up at least two hours earlier to lay the fire in Adrian's study. Grabbing her robe off the bed, she hastily shoved her arms into it and opened the door.

Adrian glowered. 'You scared the hell out of me! What's wrong? Does your head hurt?'

Not wanting to admit that it did, that she was surely suffering from some kind of delayed reaction to her impromptu detour into the ditch, that her whole body felt as though she'd been knocked down by a maraud-ing elephant, Liadan grimaced. 'I'll be okay in a min-ute. I'm sorry I overslept. Just give me a chance to jump in the shower and I'll—'

'Get back into bed.'

'What?'

'I've seen corpses with more colour than you.'

Not mincing his words or caring whether she was offended or not, Adrian strode menacingly into the room as Liadan backed feebly away towards her tumbled bed. One glance at the jumbled up bedclothes told Adrian what he'd already suspected. She'd had a bad night, a terrible one, most likely. Her pale skin looked almost translucent this morning even in the dimmed light of the room, and there were dark, telling circles beneath her drowsy eyes. He could have kicked himself for allowing her downstairs yesterday, never mind allowing her to prepare lunch and dinner for him.

'Get back into bed and stay there. I'm calling out the doctor to come and check you over. I'd take you straight to the hospital if you didn't look so damned incapable of putting one foot in front of the other right now!'

'I probably look worse than I feel.'

Desperately trying to convince him that she wasn't as feeble as she appeared, Liadan sank back down onto the bed without even realising she'd automatically done so. God, she was tired! Perhaps if she did allow herself to catch up a little with some shut-eye she would feel more like herself later on. Oh, why did this have to happen now, when she was just getting into the swing of her housekeeping role? Now Adrian would have to disrupt his schedule to tend to her and that was the last thing she wanted!

'You and I aren't going to stay friends for very long if you insist on lying to me, Liadan.' Adrian's dark gaze was ominously threatening and Liadan took a very big gulp. Was she his friend? Or was he just using a figure of speech to lure her into co-operating with his insistence that she stay in bed?

'I—I didn't want to let you down. My head's throbbing a bit but it's not bad. I think I feel worse because I didn't get much sleep last night, that's all.'

'Get beneath the covers. Come on, be quick about it, I want to phone the doctor.'

'No doctor—please!' Her blue eyes beseeched him as she threw off her robe and swung the slender legs that were hidden beneath her long white nightgown onto the bed. As she settled herself Adrian tidied the jumbled bedclothes and remade the bed. When he'd plumped up her pillows, he stood back to examine her pale, unhappy face as she stared up at him.

'You do not move from that bed unless it's to go to the bathroom; do I make myself clear?'

'I'm twenty-seven years old, not a child in kindergarten!' Her retort was mutinous and for some reason Adrian's heart squeezed unexpectedly.

'Right now you're not in a position to make intelligent decisions for yourself so I'm temporarily taking charge. Where did you get that nightgown, by the way? Your great-grandmother's attic?'

As she saw the unexpected humour in his eyes Liadan's heart did a pirouette as perfect as any prima ballerina's inside her chest. But then irritation surfaced, quickly squashing the warmer emotion. She hadn't bought the long antique nightdress to titillate anyone; it kept her warm and made her feel secure alone at night in her bed in the cottage. And what right did he have to criticise her nightwear anyway?

'What's that supposed to mean?'

'You clearly have no idea how much old-fashioned Victorian nightgowns on young, sexy, blue-eyed red-

heads turn me on.' His expression was no longer humorous, but quietly, deadly serious, and Liadan closed
her mouth on the follow-up retort she'd been going to
make. Suddenly the air in the room seemed thick and
heavy and disturbingly she felt as if she were melting
into the mattress beneath her. Unconsciously wetting
her lips, she raised her big blue eyes to nervously meet
Adrian's penetrating gaze. 'My hair isn't red. My
mother said the colour was more like strawberry-
blonde.'

'Or red-gold...like autumn leaves.'

'That's the writer in you.'

'No, Liadan.' His voice husky, Adrian's smile was
dangerously seductive. 'That's the man in me.'

It was almost uncanny how right at that instant the
pain in her head seemed to disappear. Instead, a new,
far more delightful sensation was rippling through her
body, making her feel as if she were floating on a
warm, sensuous sea, and she was no longer weighed
down by tiredness. On the contrary, she was gloriously,
vibrantly awake.

'I'll try and get some sleep. Just an hour or two, then
I should be able to come downstairs.' As much as she
desired him, Liadan badly needed him to go before
something happened that they would only regret.

'I'm still calling the doctor.'

'No, Adrian, please!' Unthinkingly, Liadan grabbed
his hand and held it. 'I'll stay in bed for the rest of the
day if you insist, but please don't call the doctor out.
I know I'm going to be fine.'

'Okay.' His dark brows drawing briefly together,
Adrian glanced down at the small, pale hand that pres-
ently held him captive and mentally fought like a
Trojan to stem the flood of sensual heat that infiltrated

his blood and aroused him as he'd never been aroused before. She wasn't well, he harshly reminded himself, so what the hell did he think he was doing lusting after her in her prim, unsuspectingly sexy Victorian night-gown? And Liadan wasn't even his girlfriend. She was the woman he'd hired to be his housekeeper—a role that was as essential to his lifestyle as his computer, and no more emotional. He knew he had to get a grip. 'Against my better judgement I won't phone the doctor. But the second you feel worse or you're in pain, that decision will rapidly change, and no argument!' Reluctantly tugging his hand free, Adrian strode to the door. 'I'll give you a couple of hours, then I'll bring you up a cup of tea.'

'You don't have to do that.'

'Get some rest. I'm going downstairs to my study to work.' His expression unreadable, he closed the door behind him without another word and Liadan had no choice but to sink back against her pillows and close her eyes.

About to go into the study at Adrian's behest, she paused outside the door for a moment, letting the tin-kling, soporific sounds of the most exquisite piano mu-sic wash over her. It was one of her favourite pieces of music, written by an Italian composer who had died an early and tragic death. Liadan knew it well and had played it often. Her throat welling with emotion as she listened, she had to shake herself out of her momentary trance to knock on the door. At Adrian's curt, 'Come in!' she pushed open the door and went inside.

He was seated by the fire in a deep leather armchair, the silver in his hair an eye-catching contrast to the darkness of his clothing, his long legs stretched out before him as though he'd been relaxing for the first time in days, and Liadan was almost loath to disturb him. His expression was closed and unsmiling as he regarded her, but right then he exuded such strength, such irrefutable male beauty, that Liadan found she could forgive him for his less than warm welcome. Besides which, he'd let her rest upstairs in her room all day and had even brought her lunch. Not all employers would be so lenient and caring to someone who'd barely been in their employ for five minutes, and she should count her blessings. She was feeling much better, too. Her headache had definitely subsided and if she didn't overdo things the following day, she would be more or less back to her old self. Now all she had to do was convince Adrian of the same.

'You must be feeling better.' He got to his feet and this time he did smile—albeit briefly. 'You've got rosy cheeks.'

Catching the ends of the dark green pashmina shawl she had teamed with her maroon sweater and long, black skirt, Liadan smiled back. 'I had a long hot bath and washed my hair and now I feel like a new woman.'

She'd left her hair free of binds this evening and it tumbled down her back in a riot of waves, like a fall of the most exquisite silk on display at a Bedouin market. For a moment Adrian was truly lost for words. The air he breathed was disturbed by the sweetly heady fragrance she wore, and its spellbinding impact registered a sensual punch deep in his belly, stirring feelings and emotions and needs he'd long trained himself to dismiss. But it was becoming more and more difficult to distance himself from this enchanting woman, he realised. He could no longer deny that he could barely think about anything other than seducing her. Even that nonsense with Petra had ceased to occupy him and last night, for the first time in ages, he hadn't dreamt about Nicole at all…

'Come and sit down.' Indicating the other chair beside the fireplace, Adrian waited for her to sit before doing so himself.

'I love this piece of music,' she enthused, wrapping her shawl more securely in front of her chest. Adrian stared. Her blue eyes sparkled like jewels in the firelight and all the gold lights in her hair seemed to dance and shimmer just for him. 'Do you play?' She directed her glance briefly across the room to the stately grand piano she had been fascinated with from the moment she'd set eyes on it.

Relaxing back into his chair, Adrian shrugged, the beginnings of a smile touching his lips. 'A little. Do you?'

'I do.' There was no point in being falsely modest, Liadan thought, not when she had been playing the piano since she was five. The only reason she hadn't gone to music school was because her parents had needed her to help them in the hotel. She could have refused, but at the end of the day she hadn't wanted to disappoint them because her brother Callum had sworn that no way was he going to go into the hotel business. So once again she had sacrificed her own needs for somebody else's… Liadan dismissed the uncomfortable thought with a slight frown between her brows.

'Would you like to play me something?' Before she could answer, Adrian moved across the room to switch off the CD that was playing.

'You don't mind?' Uncertainly Liadan got to her feet, her whole body in a state of quiet excitement at the idea of playing such a beautiful instrument.

'Be my guest.'

Settling himself back in his seat, Adrian made a steeple of his fingers and watched with interest as Liadan settled herself on the piano stool, then almost reverently lifted the lid to expose the keys. As soon as her fingers touched them she closed her eyes and began to play. The music that ensued was nothing short of wonderful. There was barely a difference from the CD recording that had been on a moment ago. The short hairs on the back of his nape standing on end, Adrian watched transfixed as Liadan continued to play, a quiet but powerful sense of excitement building slowly but inexorably inside him. Clearly at one with the music flowing from her fingertips, she kept her eyes closed mostly—as transported as he was on waves of sound so sweet, so poignant, and yet so powerful, that it almost brought tears to Adrian's eyes.

When she had finished, the silence in the room was profound. Glancing shyly across at him, Liadan smiled, her lovely face unable to conceal her joy. Without saying a word, Adrian got up and walked over to her. Taking her utterly by surprise, he bent down to capture her mouth in a long, deep, soul-stirring kiss that effectively blotted out his past as easily as though God had finally taken pity and obliterated it for good. Today was a new day. With this woman he was made anew. There was no stain on his soul to stop him completely giving himself to the moment… His hands cupping her face, feeling the strong yet delicate bones of her small jaw, Adrian explored the sensation of skin as soft as a newborn child's beneath his fingers and something settled irrevocably inside him. Something profound and good and natural that reconnected him back to a world where good things really happened. Where all was not lost in a tangled dark web of death, deceit and destruction.

Liadan could hardly believe he was kissing her. When she'd seen him approach she had secretly hoped, imagined…a peck on the cheek maybe? Something affectionate but polite that wouldn't strain the bounds of their professional relationship too much. Something to show his pleasure at her playing. But, instead, the moment his lips took possession of hers she was shaken by a deep and stirring connection that unravelled her to the core. She was still shaking. The reality of his touch was so much more satisfying and passionate than anything she could have imagined. He kissed her as if he meant it. He kissed her as if he meant that kiss to lead to so much more. Liadan shivered. Need and want and carnal longing poured into her body, filling her with a profound, restless, scalding heat that begged for fulfilment.

When his mouth finally released hers, Liadan stroked her fingers gently across her throbbing lips, her heart going wild. She could still taste him, still feel the sensuous exploration of his tongue and smell the exotically sexy tang of his aftershave.

'What was that for?' Was that really her voice? That soft bedroom huskiness?

'That was for reminding me that grace and beauty still matter in the world. Thank you.'

'You're welcome.' What else could she say? *I would gladly play for you any time, day or night, till we both grow old?*

'Where did you learn to play like that?'

'I had lessons from the age of five. I guess I never saw piano practice as a chore, as some of my friends did.' Shrugging, she carefully closed the lid on the keys and got to her feet.

Her scent was all around him—not just the fragrance she wore, but the sweet, unique lovely scent of the woman herself. *Liadan.* Even her name seemed imbued with magic. Adrian's senses were totally confounded by her. Right now he didn't even feel like putting up a fight against the soft but deadly power she wielded.

'You are an exceptional woman…you know that?'

'No, I'm not.' Glancing down awkwardly at her hands, Liadan tried to shrug his compliment off. As lovely as it was and as much as she secretly thrilled to have him bestow it, she knew it was ultimately wrong to allow this much intimacy with a man who was, after all, her employer. Somehow she was going to have to reassume the role he was paying her for as quickly as possible. No matter how much she longed to be closer to him… In a few days' time, when things got back to normal, hopefully Adrian would forget that he'd ever let his guard down so carelessly around her.

As for her own heartfelt reaction to his kiss—well, she would have to forget that, too. Adrian Jacobs' world and hers did not equate, no matter how carefully you did the maths. All of a sudden, quite uninvited, she heard Steven Ferrers' mocking voice. *He might bed you…he'll marry some posh tart whose daddy is loaded.* As much as she hated to admit it, Liadan knew he was probably right.

'With respect, if I were exceptional—what am I doing working as a housekeeper?'

'Not all exceptional people call attention to themselves, Liadan. Most go quietly about their work, doing it with honour and integrity, happy to stay out of the limelight.'

'That's true, I suppose. I wouldn't want fame if you paid me.' Tossing back her hair, Liadan grimaced. 'It certainly doesn't seem to have brought people like Petra Collins much happiness, does it?'

'You're right.' Adrian's voice was sober. 'She is a very unhappy woman and fame is definitely not all it's cracked up to be.'

'She might already be regretting dragging your name through the papers with that awful slander. Hurting you won't make her feel better. How could it?'

'Are you so quick to believe my innocence in all of this, Liadan?'

Absorbing the steady, direct perusal of his sensual dark gaze, Liadan had no hesitation in stating her feelings on the matter.

'You have too much good in you to treat someone in such a disrespectful way,' she said quietly.

Adrian was stunned by her assertion, and it painfully dawned on him that Liadan's insistence on his goodness might be pointing to deeper feelings on her part than he had realised. The thought immediately made him want to set the record straight—to disabuse her before, God forbid, she should do something so useless as to fall in love with him. If he didn't quickly destroy those hopeful illusions she had about him, he would only end up destroying her innocence more cruelly.

He reached for denial and pain—those long-time friends of his who never let him down, who reminded him exactly why he chose to live as he did, away from the public eye and away from his friends. He *deserved* the life he led. He had been complicit in the death of a beautiful young woman because of his egoism and arrogance and there was no good in him at all. None. That was why he spent his time creating shadowy, dangerous characters in his stories who lived on the periphery of life. He easily identified with the pain and self-loathing in every one of them.

'That's where you're wrong. *Very* wrong. I'm a selfish man, Liadan. I take what I want, and to hell with the consequences. As much as you might hate to hear it, Petra Collins and I were kindred spirits—that's why I don't entirely blame her for using me to further her own ends. If you believe that I kissed you because I'm nurturing some deepening affection based on the fact that you're a sweet and lovely girl, then I really have to enlighten you. I want to sleep with you. That's all. And other than getting you naked and sweaty in my bed, I need your services as a housekeeper. Sorry if that sounds brutal, but facts are facts.'

If he had lashed out at her physically, Liadan couldn't have been more shocked or more taken aback. Her mouth opened in protest to express her abhorrence of his cruel, base words, but nothing would come out. His ferocious burning glance was effectively slicing her heart in two, and in the next second he turned abruptly away as though he couldn't tolerate her company a second longer. Uttering a curse beneath his breath, he strode from the room as if suddenly there weren't enough air to breathe and he desperately needed to find some.

CHAPTER EIGHT

Two days later, as she made her way up to the topmost floor of the house to open windows and dust pictures, Liadan marvelled at the fact that she was still working for Adrian Jacobs. She was either the biggest fool who ever lived or simply some kind of martyr, because after the agony of hearing words designed to hurt her and 'enlighten' her as to what he insisted was his true character, she had wrestled with two conflicting desires. A very understandable need for self-preservation where her heart was concerned, possibly leading her to hand in her notice, and a surprisingly compelling desire to stay and tough it out—because, quite frankly, how much worse could it get? For two whole days now the atmosphere between them both had been as jagged as broken glass. When she looked at him, he looked away. When she had to ask him anything he answered her in as few words as possible. And when he'd finished speaking, his hostile brown eyes would be coldly dismissive and hurt Liadan all over again, like a rusty blade digging into a wound not yet healed.

Apart from him telling her this morning that he'd arranged for her car to be brought back from the garage 'some time today' and to insist upon taking her to the hospital himself this afternoon to have her stitches removed, their conversation had been minimal. Now the thought of having to spend time with him driving to and from the hospital was like anticipating root-canal work at the dentist.

Telling herself over and over again that he hadn't meant what he'd said, that he really *was* a good man underneath that coldly forbidding façade, Liadan forced herself to believe that she'd made the right decision in staying. And she didn't think that he used people as Petra Collins did. Adrian Jacobs was fighting demons from his past and all he was doing by assuming an air of hostility was adding another protective layer to prevent Liadan from getting close. But until he found a way to reconcile himself with the past, and see that there was light round the edges of his darkness, then he would continue to live out the rest of his life in torment.

Raising the colourful feather duster to dust down a venerable old gilt-framed print of horses and hounds off on a hunt, Liadan determinedly applied herself to the task in hand, grimacing at the very idea that things might get much worse before they got better.

'Liadan Willow? Dr Thomas will see you now.'

As she stood up to follow the slim, bright-eyed nurse into the designated room, the familiar hospital smells of disinfectant and fear making her stomach lurch, Adrian put his hand on Liadan's arm to waylay her. 'Want me to come in with you?'

Meeting his intense, concerned gaze with a little shock of surprise, she drew back her arm and shook her head. 'I'll be fine, thanks. I don't need you to hold my hand.'

Escaping before he could make some cryptic remark in response, Liadan was appalled at the ache that arose in her throat. She wasn't a coward and could handle having a few stitches removed without needing a babysitter, but, all things being equal, she wouldn't have been averse to having Adrian hold her hand. But that was before his crude remark about wanting her in his bed... Her thoughts broke off at his graphic description of *how*. Right now she wouldn't let him hold her hand if he were the last man on earth!

'Did the doctor say you'd have a scar?'

As he negotiated the purring Mercedes out of a bend in the country road, Adrian glanced sidelong at Liadan. She was staring straight ahead, her exquisite profile determinedly concentrating on the spot on the horizon where the blue-grey of the sky met the darker slate of the road. If she was being deliberately aloof, he knew he only had himself to blame. It had been a miracle that she hadn't walked out that night there and then, and, against his better judgement, Adrian had been unable to deny his relief that she hadn't. What would she think, he asked himself, if she knew it was getting to be almost torture for him to be around her? That he had deliberately distanced himself from her both mentally and physically because right now he didn't trust himself to cope with this passionate attraction that he had developed for her? That if she could see into the vivid pictures of his mind she would discover for herself his amazing proclivity for sexual fantasy as far as she was concerned? Because in all of his fantasies, Liadan was the star...

'I didn't ask. My fringe would hide it anyway.'

'Don't you care?'

'Unlike some people, I don't believe you have to be perfect to be attractive. A little scar's not going to damage me psychologically. I'm just glad I didn't do any worse damage.' To Adrian's surprise, Liadan turned her head to regard him with a steady blue gaze. 'Besides…flawed people are always more interesting, don't you think?'

What was she getting at exactly? Was she having a snipe at him, believing him to be one of those people who desired physical perfection in a mate? She couldn't be more wrong if she did, Adrian thought vehemently. What he found attractive was somebody real. Outwardly perfect good looks with nothing of substance inside left him cold.

'All right, Liadan. What's bothering you? I sense some underlying agenda here. Perhaps we should stop and talk?'

Before Liadan realised his intention, Adrian had pulled into a lay-by and switched off the engine. Now her heart started to clang like the toll of a great bell inside her chest as the small, confined space in the car seemed to grow rapidly smaller.

'I thought you didn't talk with the hired help?' she said sarcastically, blue eyes challenging him to refute her statement. For a few anxious moments she watched his hands curl around the leather-covered steering wheel as if garnering control, and she couldn't help noting the strong, well-defined knuckles and the sprinkling of dark hairs that covered them with a little jolt in her chest. Remembering how gentle his fingers had been as they'd caressed her jaw when he'd kissed her, heat rippled, unguarded, right through her body in a heady rush.

'You want me to apologise for what I said the other night?'

'If you have to ask me if I want you to, then the answer is no. I don't want you to apologise. You don't even have to put yourself out to be overly pleasant—judging by your mood the last two days, it's obviously not something that you consider a priority. But don't worry, because I can handle it. I don't need your approval or admiration to do a good job. My only stake in this relationship is the fact that I work for you and I would like to keep things that way so that I can pay my mortgage on my cottage. Simple.'

'Then let me assure you right away that you're in no danger of losing your job, Liadan. You don't think I'd willingly let go someone who can play the piano like an angel in a hurry, do you?'

Venturing a glance from beneath her curling red-gold lashes, Liadan was deeply disturbed by the fact that Adrian was smiling. Did he know what a deadly piece of weaponry in the battle of the sexes that smile was? Or how thoroughly it submerged her senses in scorching, sensual heat and guilty, guilty pleasure?

'Let me remind you, you didn't hire me to entertain you with my piano playing,' she said tartly. 'You hired me to take care of your house.'

'And *me*. Don't forget that very important little fact.'

'Perhaps what you need is a mother, in that case,' she snapped.

'What I *need*,' Adrian emphasised huskily, 'is you in my bed, Liadan. But as that would definitely be exceeding the bounds of our contract and you are obviously anxious to keep our relationship purely professional, I suppose I will have to make do with having you as my housekeeper. But I want you to know the sacrifice is killing me.'

With those wide, muscular shoulders and the devil's own twinkle in his wicked dark eyes, he was temptation personified and Liadan warned her thoughts not to speculate just *how* the sacrifice was killing him. Already she was undone just sitting beside him in the car. If she didn't make a huge effort to steer the situation into safer waters she might find herself telling him that she wouldn't mind exceeding the bounds of their contract, and then where would she be?

'We should be getting home. I've got laundry to do, and shopping and—'

'Liadan?'

'What?'

'Never mind. Let's get back, shall we?'

Changing his mind abruptly about what he'd been going to say, Adrian started the engine, then steered the car expertly out of the lay-by back onto the road. Secretly alarmed at the fact that he had almost succumbed to a very weak moment and told Liadan the cause of his torment, he congratulated himself for being strong enough to pull back. How could this pretty, inexperienced girl help him in any way other than easing a purely physical ache? She couldn't, he realised with bitterness. End of story.

'Taking the opportunity to get some fresh air, lass?' George leant against his shovel and observed her thoughtfully as Liadan came up the path towards him. Instead of her long tweed coat to keep out the cold, she wore a soft, light blue suede jacket over a white roll-necked sweater with figure-hugging black jeans. With her long hair scooped up in a very fetching top-knot, she looked as pretty as a picture to the older man's doting gaze. 'Saw Mr Jacobs drive by about ten minutes ago. Gone into town, has he?'

Glancing round at the picturesque scene that met her eyes, at rich green winter gardens that were starting to reveal their beauty now that the snow had finally gone, Liadan was more than glad that she'd ridden the storm and kept her job. If Adrian continued to maintain what he deemed a professional distance then she ought to be thankful, not unhappy. When all was said and done, no matter how much she found herself attracted to her brooding, aloof employer, she was realistic enough to know that there could be no 'happy ever after' where they were concerned. If she let herself become more intimate with him, all it would do would set up an even worse restlessness inside Liadan than she was coping with already and make her yearn for the fulfilment of a dream that was clearly impossible. She'd already wasted eighteen long months waiting for Michael to make up his mind about her—she wouldn't do the same with Adrian. Not that she believed for even a second that he would want anything more than a short, hot affair with her...

'It's such a glorious day,' she confessed, smiling, 'I couldn't resist playing hookey.'

'You're far too young to be confined to that big old house,' George agreed. 'Fancy taking a walk with me? I'll show you around a bit.'

'Oh, I'd love that!' Liadan enthused, her heart lifting at the prospect.

The gardens stretched much further afield than she had ever imagined. Path after path revealed something new—treasures like the orangery, a grotto with hundreds upon hundreds of seashells embedded deep within its walls, and winter blooms including snowdrops and crocuses in breathtaking abundance. Enchanted at nearly every turn, Liadan forgot her cares and concerns as she completely succumbed to the magic of Adrian's gardens and George's quietly authoritative garden lore.

'People often make the mistake of thinking they can

control the garden, but what they soon learn is that the garden controls them. It takes you over completely. Watering, weeding, digging, pruning, spraying, it becomes an obsession after a while. One I wouldn't willingly give up and that's the truth.'

'I can tell that you love it,' Liadan commented with a smile, 'but don't you find all this work a bit much for just yourself and your son?'

Somehow, Liadan couldn't bring herself to say 'Steven'. She was still wary and smarting from their last upsetting encounter. Thankfully, he didn't seem to be around today, either. Her blue eyes darted from side to side just to check.

'Funny you should bring that up. I've had a touch of the old arthritis in my knees for the past few months and I was going to mention to Mr Jacobs how I could probably do with another hand around the place to help. Specially leading up to spring. There's a lot to be done.'

'Then you should definitely mention it. I'm sure he'd be only too willing to get you the help you need, George.'

'I'm sure you're right, lass. Perhaps I will have a talk with him. To tell you the truth, I don't think Steven is a natural gardener. He's got his mind on too many other useless things, that boy.'

Perfectly understanding why George had reservations about the younger man's commitment levels, Liadan nodded in sympathy.

'Thanks for showing me around, George. It's been a great way to spend an illicit half-hour. I've had a lovely time. Best go in now, though; I need to think about what I'm going to do for dinner.'

'You go ahead, lass. Feel free to walk about the

place whenever you feel the need. I'm always around
if you need to know anything about the garden. By the
way, I'm glad that story about Mr Jacobs has died
down in the papers. She's a bad 'un, that Collins
woman, for telling such lies.' Tipping his hat, George
looked distant for a moment before he jammed his
hands into the big patch pockets of his jerkin and
headed back down the terracotta bricked path he had
walked with Liadan.

Careful not to dislodge any of the papers that littered
Adrian's writing table, Liadan picked up the drained
cup and saucer and added it to the tray she'd left on
the piano. She was about to vacate the study when she
caught a glimpse of an opened newspaper jutting out
from the side of the desk that Adrian had his computer
on, and instinctively moved towards it.

'Actress retracts abortion claim,' she read with
thumping heart, alongside a picture of Adrian and his
solicitor Edward Barry, taken outside on that awful day
when reporters had camped out on his doorstep. Putting
down the tray, Liadan sat down in the leather chair
opposite the desk and read further. When she got to
the part where she learned that Petra Collins and
Adrian had comforted each other after her divorce and
the brutal, untimely death of Adrian's fiancée Nicole
Wilson, in a terrorist attack on a foreign embassy, she
let the paper flutter down unheeded into her lap.

Staring into space for a long moment to gather her
thoughts, Liadan felt vindicated in the flood of relief
and shock that swept through her body. His fiancée had
been killed. That was why he had locked himself away
from the rest of humanity, and that was no doubt why
he was so bitter. Liadan didn't have to be a genius to

know that Adrian blamed himself for Nicole's death. She also didn't have to read the words a little further down the page where Adrian had been quoted at the time of the attack as saying, 'It should have been me,' to know that he made himself entirely responsible for what had happened to his fiancée.

On top of that, she read that Petra Collins was 'extremely regretful' that she'd taken 'wrong advice' and spitefully embellished her brief liaison with Adrian Jacobs to further her own career. Liadan's relief knew no bounds. Adrian was innocent of all the slander that had been directed towards him, including his own bitter assertion that he was responsible for his fiancée's death. Despite his savage denial to the contrary, he *was* a good man…

The echo of the doorknocker resounding through the house just then made Liadan jerk round in shock. Quickly gathering up the paper, folding it, then placing it carefully beside the computer, she went back to the piano to fetch her tray, then hurried out of the study, down the corridor and out into the hall.

Leaving the tray on a little cherry-wood side table that was home to a beautiful Chinese-style patterned vase, she patted down her wayward hair, straightened the hem of her sweater and went to answer the door.

'Can I come in?'

'I—no, you can't! What is it, Mr Ferrers? What do you want this time?'

Staring into Steven Ferrers' defiant gaze, she suddenly felt as if her stomach had a lead weight inside it. As the distinct smell of sour alcohol floated up to her nostrils Liadan's fingers curled more tightly round the edges of the door, all her senses on red alert.

'You and I need to have a little talk, Miss *Willow*.' He drawled her name as if it disgusted him and the fingers of chilling cold fear that had crept round her skin grew immediately icier.

'I'm sorry, but I have nothing to say to you. Now if you'll just let me—'

The force of his hand grabbing the door and jerking it wide almost sent Liadan flying. As she struggled to right herself Steven swept through the door and pinned her against the wall, his face pressed dangerously close to her own so that the sour smell of booze wafting down at her almost made her sick.

'Let me go! What the hell do you think you're doing?'

'Ice princess, that's what you are…just the type that gets my goat. Think you're too good for someone like me, don't you? You'd rather consort with the likes of that murderer Jacobs!'

'What are you talking about? He's not a murderer!' Shoving against his chest with all her might, Liadan made little impression on Steven Ferrers' strength. He was slim but hard muscled and she was no match for him. She knew it with a sinking heart. No matter how much she pushed and shoved, he wasn't going to let her go…

'Said he was responsible for killing his girlfriend, didn't he? Said he went back to the Jeep and left her there on the pavement for a bomb to kill her!'

'That doesn't make him a murderer, you idiot! Now let me go before you get into real trouble. If your father finds out he'll be—'

'Bitch!' At the mention of his father, Steven's eyes narrowed to two menacing slits and with no warning he raised his hand and struck Liadan hard across the

face. As she reeled from the blow tears started to her
eyes and her heart started to pump with stark, cold
dread. There was no one around to hear her call for
help, she realised. Adrian had gone out and George
could have been anywhere. The gardens were huge and
rambling. If he was in one of the greenhouses he'd be
even less likely to hear her shouts for help.

'You asked for it, princess. You should have been
nicer to me and then you wouldn't have got hurt.' His
words slurred, Steven put his face closer to hers, paying
no attention to her continuing struggle to free herself.
Spying the large ceramic vase on the table she'd set
the tray on, just inches away from where she stood,
Liadan saw a sudden chance to get away. But Steven
was pinning her arms to her side as he tried to kiss her
and she couldn't free them.

She would have to try another tack. The chances of
it working might be slim, but she had to try because
the consequences if she didn't hardly bore contempla-
tion.

'You're right,' she breathed huskily, lowering her
voice. 'I should have been nicer to you. You're right.
It does get lonely out here. A girl needs—a girl needs
someone to keep her warm.'

'That's better. I knew you could be sweet if you
wanted to. Now stop talking and kiss me.'

'You're holding me too tightly. Just let me free my
hands, will you? I can wrap my arms around your neck
and k-kiss you much better.' Barely daring to breathe,
Liadan tried to make her eyes look wide and seductive
as she forced herself to smile up into Steven's threatening eyes. Would he fall for her little ruse? God help
her if he didn't... Her face still burning from his blow,

she'd never prayed harder for divine intervention than she did at that moment.

Miraculously, Steven briefly let her go. In what seemed an interminably long split second, Liadan immediately reached out to the side for the vase, grabbed it and brought it crashing down on the side of his skull. With a drunken groan he clutched his head before sliding bonelessly down to the black and white checked floor, and, without another glance, Liadan made herself run for all she was worth out of the house.

CHAPTER NINE

WHEN Adrian saw Liadan run down the stone steps that led from the house and turn onto the drive, looking desperately around her, his heart jumped right into his throat. Parking the Mercedes in record time on the gravel, he leapt out of the driver's seat and raced towards her.

'Liadan! What happened?'

When he reached her and witnessed the livid red welt bruising her pale cheek, her lovely hair coming undone from its fastening and her blue eyes huge and damp with tears, he naturally dragged her hard against his chest and held her. Feeling her slender body shake almost uncontrollably in his arms, he put her a little away from him and stared down questioningly into her eyes. 'What the hell happened?'

'I think I've killed Steven Ferrers.' Her lower lip trembling, Liadan's face grew even paler apart from the vivid red welt. Something in the pit of Adrian's stomach went sickly cold.

'How? Where is he now?'

'He's in the hall. I hit him, Adrian. I hit him with a vase and he fell to the floor.'

'Wait here.' His mind racing overtime, he briefly touched his fingers to Liadan's unmarked cheek before running towards the steps that led into the house, negotiating them two at a time until he disappeared inside the entrance. Unable to heed his command to stay where she was, Liadan followed him, albeit more slowly, dreading the confrontation with what could possibly be Steven Ferrers' dead body.

But when she reached the door and slowly walked inside, Adrian had a very much alive and kicking Steven slammed up against the far wall, his fist raised bare inches from the other man's blood-stained face. After her initial relief of finding her assailant still breathing, everything inside Liadan went deathly cold at the idea that Adrian might finish the job she'd started. The rage coming off those broadly muscular shoulders of his in his tanned leather flying jacket was tangible and she was frightened of the damage he might do in the grip of it.

'Adrian! No! Don't hurt him!'

As he turned briefly to look at her Adrian's dark gaze was malevolent. 'He's lucky he's not dead already if he did that to you. Did he do that to your face?' he barked.

'Let him go and we'll talk,' she pleaded, more fearful for the damage that might be done to Adrian's already much maligned reputation than any harm that could be inflicted on Steven Ferrers.

'Oh, we'll talk, all right. Come here and get my mobile phone out of my jacket pocket. I'm not risking letting this lowlife go until the police get here.'

'The police?' The sudden rush of blood to her head made Liadan momentarily lose her bearings. 'Adrian, think about it. You don't want to involve the police in this. You know what the papers will do to you. They'll put some poisonous slant on it to make you look bad. Just let him go, will you? I'm all—I'm all right, I promise!'

Adrian couldn't believe she was thinking about his reputation when she'd been attacked by the scum he currently had up against the wall. His chest hurt abominably when he thought about what she had been through. Why the hell had he decided to go into town today of all days?

'Please, Adrian. He's bleeding. I—I hit him hard with that vase.'

The shattered pieces of the pretty Chinese vase were scattered everywhere. For one brief, hysterical moment Liadan wondered whether it might be a Ming or something equally valuable. Heaven knew Adrian's lovely house was filled to the rafters with antiques and expensive objets d'art of all descriptions.

With a ripe curse Adrian let go of the other man, only to have him ignominiously slide down the wall and sit on the floor groaning as he held his hand to his head. With none-too-gentle fingers Adam made a perfunctory examination of the wound, then, straightening, walked across the chequered floor to Liadan.

'He'll live, more's the pity. He's cut but it doesn't look like it needs stitching. More to the point, how are you?' Wincing, he touched the livid red welt with his fingertips, his chest growing tighter by the second at the realisation that she'd been hurt…and under his roof, where she should have been safe. He cursed the day that he had gone against all his instincts and employed Steven Ferrers as a favour to his father. No doubt when his faithful head gardener learned of what had happened, it would break his heart. But right now it was Liadan and only Liadan that Adrian was interested in.

'Now listen to me,' he said firmly, tenderly pushing away a curling tendril of spun red-gold away from her brow. 'I want you to go into the kitchen and wait for me there. I don't want you to do anything but sit and wait for me, is that clear?'

Suddenly too weary to argue, Liadan nodded mutely.

'As soon as I've dealt with him—' he jerked his head disparagingly in Steven's direction '—I'll come and join you. Now go along and don't worry.'

'You won't hurt him?' She bit her lip, her blue eyes looked enormous in her small, oval face.

'I may be as mad as hell but I know the risks, Liadan. I'm going to phone George on his mobile and get him over here, then I'll take things from there.'

'Okay…if you're sure?'

With one reluctant glance back at Steven Ferrers slumped pitifully against the wall, Liadan walked with relief back to the kitchen.

Half an hour had never seemed so long. As she sat at the kitchen table nursing the deliberately sweet cup of tea she'd forced herself to make Liadan flinched at every sound she wasn't sure of, fearing the worst when she heard nothing and straining her ears for any sign of Adrian returning. When she heard a door finally slam somewhere in the house, she started to get to her feet, anxious to know who was leaving, terrified in case Adrian had decided to go for the police after all and had left Steven sitting on the floor in the hall. But when Adrian himself came through the door, shucked his jacket off those reassuringly broad shoulders of his and stood regarding her with deep concern in his eyes, Liadan had never known such sweet and blessed relief.

'What's happened? Did George come? Is he taking Steven to the hospital?'

'George came. He's taking Steven home to let him sleep off his drunken stupor. We both took another look at his head wound and it's nothing to worry about.

It certainly doesn't warrant a hospital visit and, even if it did, I'm sure Steven would rather avoid any kind of authorities right now in the light of what he did.'

'And how is George?'

'How do you think?' Shaking his head, Adrian came over to Liadan, studying her gravely as she sat in the ladder-backed kitchen chair, her hands cupped round her drink. 'He's appalled, ashamed, furious and ready to do his son some serious damage. His only fear is that whatever he says or does won't sink in. Steven's been in trouble with the police before, Liadan. Petty thieving, a couple of pub brawls…nothing too serious up until now.' Leaning back against the table, Adrian put out his hand and tipped up her chin. Her face was drained of colour apart from the red mark on her cheek and she looked as if she'd been crying again.

He blamed himself completely for what had happened. He had hired Steven Ferrers knowing he had a criminal record, even if he had done it as a favour to George. George, who wouldn't even help himself to a glass of water unless it was offered first. Now Liadan had been hurt for the second time in a few days. Could anyone blame Adrian for believing that he and this house were some sort of jinx for the woman?

'I should get you some brandy for shock.' Reluctantly he withdrew his hand, inwardly fighting against an almost insurmountable need to keep on touching her and never stop.

'I made some sweet tea. It does the same thing, I heard.'

'How did he get in?' His logical mind demanding he know all the answers and tie up any loose or suspicious ends, Adrian was still having trouble quelling the tumult of emotion that was crowding his chest.

Truth to tell, if he couldn't tear Steven Ferrers limb from limb, he wanted to break something instead...do anything that would divert the maelstrom of anger that was almost suffocating him.

'He knocked on the door. Before I realised he had been drinking, he just pushed back the door and came inside.'

Replacing her cup back in its saucer, Liadan pushed her fingers agitatedly through her hair, dislodging her tortoiseshell clasp completely. Her hair cascaded down over her shoulders, making her small, oval face appear disconcertingly like a child's.

'What did he say?'

'What did he say?' Liadan repeated through numbed lips. With great reluctance she forced herself to remember. She didn't really want to talk about what had happened at all. All she really wanted to do was forget the whole horrible incident had ever occurred. But staring up into Adrian's hard, implacable face, she knew he wasn't going to let her do that. If this had happened in his house in another day and age, no doubt he would have challenged the other man to a duel in defence of Liadan's honour. The thought almost made her smile, but just as quickly she wanted to cry. Adrian's only concern for her was that she had been hurt. It would be foolish indeed to delude herself he would come to her rescue for any reason other than what decency dictated. She was his employee and, naturally, like any other employer with integrity, he wanted to assure himself that everything possible was done to alleviate her distress.

'Um...he said that I was an ice princess. That I thought myself too good for him.'

'He'd come on to you before?'

Feeling almost overwhelmingly tired, Liadan shrugged. 'Being the kind of man he seems to be, I suppose he couldn't help himself when I'm the nearest female for miles around.'

It was hard for Adrian to believe she could be so self-deprecating. Didn't she have any idea just how beautiful she was? How much any red-blooded heterosexual male would look at her and fantasise about making her his?

Seeing the telling muscle flinch in his jaw, Liadan thought it best to keep quiet about just how much Steven Ferrers had frightened her—and not just today when his threats had finally tipped over into actual physical violence. The sting of that slap suddenly stealing into the edges of her consciousness, she couldn't help but shudder. If that vase hadn't been so close to hand, if she hadn't had the chance to bring it down upon his head and steal the opportunity to escape... The possibility didn't bear thinking about. An overwhelming urge to be at home in her little cottage, to light the fire and sit by it with Izzy on her lap, to be safe and warm again, swept through her with such force that her body prepared itself immediately for flight. Unable to conceal her longing for home, she looked straight at Adrian and told him exactly what was on her mind.

'I need to go back home for a while. Do you understand? I need to be by myself and try to make myself feel better. Is that okay with you?'

Understanding her need and yet dreading being alone in the house without her, Adrian nodded reluctantly. The evidence of her presence—both physical and intangible—was all around, impressing itself upon him and the house almost indelibly, like invisible golden cobwebs that he couldn't brush away. Without her both he and the house would be stark, empty shells.

'Whether it's okay or not with me, I know it's what you need to do. Go and pack some things, then. I'll come and carry your bag to the car for you when you're ready. I'm not letting you drive yourself. I'll take you.' To Liadan's surprise, he was gone from the room before she even had the chance to rise up out of her chair.

'Come on then, Izzy. Come and finish this lovely salmon left over from my dinner…even though you're getting impossibly fat!' Admiring the gusto with which her beloved pet was tucking into her unexpected treat, Liadan lifted her gaze to glance round her warm, snug kitchen with something akin to contentment. After two days of being back home, with her own things around her—not least Izzy and the old Victorian piano she had haggled for at a local auction—her spirits had definitely started to heal. The only sting in the tail was the fact that Adrian wasn't with her.

She missed him. Missed him with a slow, burning ache in her chest that felt as if it would never heal. When he had dropped her off at the cottage two days ago he had declined to come in. Instead he'd left her bag on the porch step and backed away as though he couldn't escape quickly enough. His face had appeared coldly distant once again, even when he'd insisted on her assurance before he left that she would be all right on her own and didn't need him to call someone to come and be with her. Then he had climbed into his Jeep, gunned the engine, and sped off down the small country lane as if he had a posse of trigger-happy mercenaries on his tail.

Returning to her living room and settling herself in

the cosy nook before the fire, Liadan picked up the book she had been half-heartedly trying to read, telling herself that tomorrow she would go back to the house and resume work. That was, if Adrian hadn't decided in the interim that it was more trouble than it was worth keeping her on. Even now in her absence he could be interviewing other prospective candidates for her job. The thought made her heart stall. If she didn't work for him any more, what excuse would she have to ever see him again? He was a high-profile, well-known author and she was... Well. She was twenty-seven years old, possibly without a job and alone again. She eased the sudden aching cramp in her throat with a harsh breath.

When the echo of the doorknocker rudely broke into her thoughts, she jerked her head round in alarm, knocking her book off her lap and watching it land on the floor with a spine-jingling thud. As it was nearly ten o'clock in the evening, she told herself she had good reason to be alarmed. What if Steven Ferrers had somehow found out where she lived? What if he wanted to punish her for what she had done in her own defence? Clutching the white towelling robe that she had donned straight after her bath tightly round her, she padded barefoot across the carpet to the white-panelled door, then peeped cautiously out through the spy-hole. Her startled gaze settled on the face that had been occupying most of her thoughts from morning through till night—albeit looking as stern as she'd ever seen him and soaked through to the skin from the pounding rain—and Liadan's fingers shook uncontrollably as she turned the key and lifted the latch.

'Adrian! What are you doing here?'

She couldn't believe she was shaking so. Trembling

because his sudden, unexpected presence was almost too much to bear...

'Are you going to invite me in or do I have to stand here getting even wetter?' There was no answering smile, no teasing lift of a dark brow, just a scowl that would put the fear of God into a grizzly bear. Feeling strangely light-headed, Liadan stood back to let him enter.

'I'm sorry, I wasn't thinking. I'll get you a towel.'

She was back in an instant, pressing a large pink towel into his hands, then anxiously standing back while he unzipped his dark green waterproof, shook it off and hung it on the hook at the back of the door where Liadan's bright orange scarf presently hung.

'It's a foul night out there.' Roughly drying his sodden hair, he combed his fingers through it almost impatiently, then threw the towel on the arm of the nearest chair.

'You didn't come by car?'

'I decided I needed the walk.'

That explained why the sound of the doorknocker had taken her so much by surprise. Moving automatically across to the fire, he held out his hands to the flickering flames, his expression suggesting he was lost for a moment in the pictures he seemed to find there. The room was alive with his presence, the air crackling with electricity. The plain fact of the matter was that he would be impossible to ignore, no matter where he was. His strong, muscular physique was both reassuring and awesome at the same time, and right now Liadan was more awed than reassured. Studying him for a long moment without speaking, secretly appraising every fascinating inch of him as though her gaze had been starved of his presence for too long, she couldn't help but release a sigh.

'How are you?'

He turned to examine her, his dark gaze more probing than the most powerful microscope, seemingly stripping her of every secret she ever had, his relentless study making everything inside her drown in heat. Automatically touching her fingers to her cheek, Liadan withdrew them again just as quickly, in case he thought she was looking for sympathy.

'I'm fine. Luckily I don't bruise easily.'

Scanning the flush that brought a revealing rose pink to her cheeks, Adrian was not so easily placated. Yesterday and today he'd suffered agonies of doubt and fear wondering how she was—whether after this appalling incident she would want to come back to his house at all. Finally, unable to stand the tension of not knowing any longer and disparagingly dismissing the phone as a less-than-adequate method of communication, he'd donned his waterproof, stepped out into the rain and headed to her cottage to confront her. For a man working to an impossible deadline, he reminded himself, it was crazy behaviour.

'Can I get you a drink or something? I've got some brandy if you want something a bit stronger than tea or coffee. You must be cold after being out in the rain.'

Ignoring her question, Adrian asked what he was most desperate to learn. 'When are you intending coming back to work?'

To his relief, her blue eyes didn't slide away in avoidance of the question. 'Tomorrow, actually. I was thinking of coming back in the morning, if that's all right with you?'

'Of course it's all right with me! Why wouldn't it be?'

'I thought you might have decided to hire somebody else in my absence. I wouldn't have blamed you. I know your work is very important and you need somebody reliable to—'

'Do you honestly think for one moment that I would go behind your back and hire someone else when the reason you've come back home is because you were assaulted by someone who worked for me?'

Clearly exasperated, Adrian dragged his fingers irritably through his damp hair, his expression almost feral. Liadan couldn't take her eyes off him at the realisation that, despite needing a reliable housekeeper to take care of the house while he worked, he wouldn't even consider employing someone else in her absence. Even if it meant that things were difficult for him.

'You seem so angry, and I don't understand why.'

'I'm not angry with you, Liadan, even though it might seem that way. I'm merely furious with myself for hiring Steven Ferrers in the first place. For that appalling error of judgement I can't forgive myself.'

'You already blame yourself for far too much, Adrian.' Her hands itched to reach out and comfort him and her body ached to hold him, but Liadan forced herself to stand her ground even though to be so near and yet so far was pure torment…

'What do you mean?' His dark gaze bemused, he stared at her.

She realised with horror that she'd been about to blurt out what she'd read in his newspaper about Nicole's death. About the fact that he believed *he* should have died instead, that her death was somehow his fault. Instinctively knowing that that would have been just about the worst move she could make, because he wasn't a man who would willingly admit to vulnerability in any way, Liadan furiously back-pedalled.

'I only meant that it wasn't your fault that Steven did what he did. We're all responsible for our own actions, aren't we?'

Hovering in the narrow doorway of the kitchen, Liadan smoothed her hands nervously down the front of her robe, unwittingly dislodging the material covering her chest. Adrian stared, dry-mouthed. The sensual globe of one perfect breast was almost revealed in its entirety. As heat careened straight into his groin and ignited desire almost too violent to be tamped, he nearly forgot his own name. With her long red-gold hair curling prettily over her shoulders and clearly wearing nothing but that virginal white robe, she was like one of the sirens from Greek mythology. Only it wasn't just her soft, sweet voice that was luring him. Everything about Liadan aroused his excitement, from the way she moved her slender yet curvaceous body, to her naturally compassionate and loving nature.

Her loveliness enticed him to a temptation so great that it was impossible for him to think about anything else other than getting her naked as soon as he could and showing her in no uncertain terms just what she did to him. If he was honest, wasn't it desire that had driven him out in the foulest of weathers to seek her? He'd needed to see her. He desperately needed to be in the same room as her and breathe the same air…

'Come here.'

'Why?' Following his burning glance, Liadan gasped when she saw what he was looking at. Covering herself immediately, she silently cursed her lack of finesse. *Damn!* She should have thought about throwing on some clothes before answering the door. Now Adrian was making her unravel simply by looking at her, the carnal longing in his eyes brazen and unmistakable. What could he do to her already-quivering body if he touched her as if he meant it? Just as every inch of her was aching for him to do?

'If you don't come over here, Liadan…I'll just have to come over there.'

She knew he was serious. Knew it in every tingling fibre of her being. Just as she knew she was too weak to deny him…didn't *want* to deny him because she'd been craving his attention this way for too long…

'What is it?' Moving to stand in front of him on legs that felt as though she stood on the deck of a ship in a storm, she dared to meet the naked invitation in his disturbing dark eyes.

'You can ask me that when I'm so consumed by my longing for you that I can't think about anything else?'

There was a sharp intake of breath. Whether it was his or hers, Liadan couldn't have said for sure. But when he curled his fingers round the edges of her robe and with one sure, firm tug exposed her breasts to his hungry, rapacious glance, the long, shuddering sigh that followed was definitely her own.

'I want to touch you. I want to touch you everywhere,' he growled. Then, lowering his mouth to one exposed breast, he took her deep inside his scalding heat and suckled her hard. Liadan's slender hips bucked against him and in the next breath she was anchoring her fingers in his thick, dark hair, moaning his name and letting him push the rest of her robe from her shoulders so that she stood naked in his arms. Her craving to touch him was as passionate and rapacious as his. Desire was like a molten, flowing river pulsing unstoppably through her veins, carrying her relentlessly along with no help for it but to submit completely to its power.

Hands shaking, she helped him remove his black wool sweater, frustrated at fingers and thumbs that wouldn't work quickly enough. Then, unadulterated pleasure rolling through her at the sight of his wonderful masculine chest, she looked her fill. He had biceps of steel and abdominal muscles of iron and Liadan ran her fingers across his flat, male nipples and would have bent her head to kiss him there had he not swept her high into his arms and carried her to the armchair. With a secret little smile playing maddeningly around his irresistibly sexy mouth, he positioned her in his lap so that he had full access to her breasts and her mouth. Then, capturing her lips in a hard, hot kiss, he unzipped his jeans, sheathed himself with the protection he'd produced from his back pocket and thrust deeply inside her.

For a moment Liadan truly thought she saw stars. In her wildest, most uninhibited dreams she'd never dreamt a man's possession could be like this…so hot, so untamed and so unbelievably, exquisitely perfect. As Adrian's hands guided her hips down upon him in deeply rhythmic, sensuous motion she was suddenly ferociously glad that she hadn't slept with Michael.

'You're so beautiful,' he told her with a heated, possessive glance. 'A golden girl. So…hot and…tight…' As much as he prided himself on making sure his lover had just as good a time as he did, Adrian knew without a shadow of a doubt it wouldn't be long before this lovely, fascinating girl took him over the edge. Her body was sinfully beautiful. She surprised him with a wanton sensuality that he could hardly have believed, her long hair flowing over her lovely satiny breasts as she bent her head once more to receive his kiss, and Adrian knew he wouldn't easily be able to give her up when the time came. The thought made him thrust even more deeply inside her as if staking a claim for all eternity and Liadan cried out as Adrian felt the hot, rhythmic contractions of her muscles holding him fast. Then he was quickly following her, groaning out loud with the ecstasy of it as his body succumbed to wave after wave of the most turbulent, erotic pleasure known to man.

CHAPTER TEN

'ARE you sure you wouldn't like a hot drink?'

Liadan was wrapped up once again in her soft towelling robe, and her glance was nervous as she watched Adrian reaching for his waterproof at the back of the door. Although she hadn't really expected him to stay the night, she still couldn't help feeling hurt that he was leaving so abruptly after their passionate union. But she wasn't insensitive to the fact that there had been a definite cooling in his manner towards her since he had got dressed, and now she was going through the torments of hell wondering why.

'I need to get back. I have to work.'

Scraping his fingers through his hair, he managed a smile of sorts: a smile that barely reached the suddenly frigid depths of his unsettling brown eyes. Liadan's hand fluttered nervously to her throat.

'Adrian, I hope you don't—'

'It's not you, Liadan. I don't want to hurt you but if you were expecting something more...' He shrugged his wide shoulders and grimaced. 'To be brutal, sex is all I can offer you. I just can't give you anything more meaningful than that. You're a lovely girl and some day you'll no doubt meet the right man who'll fulfil all your expectations of love and romance...but that's not me, sweetheart. That's not me.'

As he turned and opened the door the wind rushed in with a vengeance, bringing with it a spray of ice-cold rain that made Liadan shiver violently beneath her inadequate robe. But it wasn't just the freezing rain that made her blood run cold. It was the bleak, haunted look in Adrian's eyes that was taking him even further away from her than physical distance ever could.

'They're beautiful, George, thank you.'

Liadan dropped her gaze to the abundant bunch of daffodils George had just presented her with. Her heart went out to the older man. As he stood in the front hall, his cap in his hand, his embarrassment was plain to see, and clearly painfully acute. Liadan had already planned on visiting him this morning to put his anxieties at rest, to assure him that she didn't blame him in any way for what his son had done. But she hadn't yet had the opportunity, because Adrian had had a long list of things for her to do on her return.

He obviously thought that if he kept her as busy as possible she wouldn't have time to brood on whether she'd made the right decision to come back or not. He was wrong.

Although they'd shared the ultimate intimacy, he'd made it perfectly clear that she wasn't to expect much else, and, although Liadan was heartsick about such a decision, she couldn't bring herself to leave. Not when she now knew with all certainty that she loved him more than she could ever imagine loving anyone else on this earth... They had a deep connection—even if Adrian was too blind to see it. She didn't buy that 'all he could offer her was sex' baloney. He was merely hiding behind that harsh assertion to prevent himself from ever being emotionally hurt again. Liadan knew that as surely as she knew her own name.

So, even now when Adrian was already laying down new ground rules as to how he expected their relationship to continue, Liadan was determined to stay put and weather the storm. Did he regret making love to her last night? The mere idea scared her senseless. If only there were some way of getting through to him, of proving to him that she would never let him down or break his heart…

She tried to convince herself that what really mattered, practically speaking, was that she still had a job and would be able to meet her mortgage payments. But she knew she'd be willing to live in a tent if it meant that she could be with the man that she loved for ever.

'Nothing I could say or do could make it up to you, lass…for what Steven did.' George lifted his head as though determined to face whatever punishment Liadan cared to mete out, and his pale blue eyes went strangely glassy when she merely smiled and pressed his hand warmly with her own.

'You don't owe me anything, George. You aren't responsible for what your son did. He's an adult. I certainly don't think we should let it come between our friendship, do you?'

'That's very good of you, lass…more than I deserve. You know Mr Jacobs fired him, of course? I'm only grateful that he didn't call the police, even though the stupid little bugger deserved it—pardon my language. I just wanted to reassure you that he wouldn't be bothering you again. I've paid for him to go and stay with my sister Marge for a while down in Wales. Her and her husband are farmers and they'll keep him busy, don't you worry. He knows if he ever sets foot up here again, *I'll* be the first one to call the police.'

'All right, George. I'm sure you must have plenty of

work to be getting on with—particularly now when we're short-staffed. Liadan has work to do, too.'

Adrian walked up beside her, taking her by surprise, his tone ringing icy command and clearly expecting those commands to be instantly met. As she glanced sidelong at his formidably stern profile her stomach clenched hard at the pain of the little knot that was currently twisting her insides together.

Placing his cap back firmly on his head, George muttered, 'I'll be seeing you then, lass,' and stepped rigidly back as though every inch of his body were covered in painful bruises. When he had gone, Adrian shut the doors firmly behind him, surveying Liadan with a cool regard as if the intimacy they had shared had never even taken place.

'I'd find a vase to put those in and get on with lunch if I were you. My editor's coming to see me this afternoon so I'm going to be pretty tied up for the rest of the day.'

Liadan had trouble swallowing down her shock and outrage—at his cavalier treatment of George as well as at the cold disdain with which he all but ordered her back to work. She felt as though she were having a bad dream. Her hands were clutching the daffodils too tightly, and her candid blue eyes couldn't disguise her hurt and disappointment.

'Did you have to speak to George so roughly? The poor man is obviously going through agonies over his son.'

'The *poor man's* son assaulted you in *my* house!' Adrian snapped back through gritted teeth. 'I would be perfectly within my rights to sack him too, under the circumstances!'

Unable to bite back the gasp that came to her lips,

Liadan stared in disbelief. 'You wouldn't be so cruel, surely? George has worked here a long time and as far as I know he's done a wonderful job. Where would he go? What would he do?'

'That's not my concern.'

'Then what *is* your concern, Adrian, if you don't mind my asking?' Clutching the flowers tightly to her chest, Liadan finally couldn't halt the flow of anger that was bubbling up inside her. The man wasn't an automaton…he had to feel something, didn't he? It wasn't human not to feel anything at all. 'All I can say is that it must be very cold in that empty place inside your chest where your heart should be. You seem to think you can protect yourself from every bit of hurt and trouble by shutting off all your feelings and emotions like a tap. But nobody can pretend not to feel things, Adrian. Not even you!'

'I don't have time for this pointless conversation. Just get on with your work, will you, and leave my feelings out of this?' With a contemptuous glare that made Liadan feel as if an icy wind had just swept over her, he strode away as if the matter were completely at an end.

He hadn't been able to concentrate on a damn thing that Lynne Scott, his editor, had said and he certainly couldn't share in her excitement that, in her opinion, his current work in progress was going to be his biggest and most lucrative book yet. Truth to tell, Adrian had fallen completely out of love with the damned thing. When he should have been all fired up because he was so very near the graphically gruesome shock ending he'd been planning on, all he could think about was his lust for his pretty housekeeper.

Making love with Liadan had been amazing. The sexual drought he'd deliberately imposed upon himself after the messy entanglement with Petra couldn't have been more thoroughly or satisfyingly brought to an end as it had been last night in Liadan's cottage. Whenever Adrian closed his eyes—even briefly—all he could see were those sensuously darkened blue eyes of hers, all her feelings bruisingly laid bare as she gave herself to him over and over until he was sated.

To speak to her as coldly as he had done, to treat her almost with contempt when she had so readily jumped to George's defence this morning, had been both despicable and unforgivable. But Adrian was still furious about that whole business with Steven Ferrers, uncontrollably enraged that Liadan had been hurt under his roof when he should have been there to protect her. Just as he should have been there to take the consequences of that explosion instead of Nicole...

Cursing out loud as he pushed out of his chair, he strode out of the room, determined to take a walk under the stars and to quell the rising sense of panic that was threatening to engulf him.

Hearing the front doors slam, Liadan paused in the task of removing her make-up. She glanced down at the slim gold wrist-watch she'd taken off and left on the edge of the sink, and saw that it was just after midnight. Didn't the man believe in rest? Biting her lip and telling herself she must be some kind of masochist, she put down the cotton-wool pad she'd started to use and went back into the bedroom. She didn't really know what she intended or whether she was actually going to make matters worse, but she pulled her short sheep-skin jacket from the wardrobe, quickly stuck her stockinged feet into black leather loafers and hurried down-stairs to the ground floor.

Bathed in moonlight, the gardens were an ethereal, magical place. As Liadan adjusted her gaze to the moonlit paths her heart raced a little as she searched for Adrian. She knew that the gardens were full of secret little places to make oneself scarce, and she realised she had a task on her hands if she was to find him. But find him she would. After his pleasant-looking editor had left, the atmosphere in the house had been as if somebody had just died. The weight of the gloom that had descended was making Liadan feel jumpy and miserable.

She might be determined to weather the storm, but how was she supposed to work when Adrian could hardly bring himself to speak to her with a civil tongue? Was he angry because he believed she might have some expectations where he was concerned? Especially now because they'd made love? Her sigh making a little cloud of her breath in the chill night air, Liadan shivered and turned up the warm collar of her jacket to ward off the cold.

'What the hell do you think you're doing out here alone?'

'Don't do that! You almost gave me a heart attack!'

Her blue eyes huge, almost luminous in the moonlight, Liadan stumbled backwards in shock as Adrian came up beside her. Grabbing her arm tightly, he pulled her hard against his chest without thinking—his reaction automatic and unequivocal. Staring down into her startled face, he laughed harshly.

'You should take better care where you wander. This garden is full of ghosts that only come out at night.'

Liadan believed him. Feeling his grip on her arm

tighten with no indication that he intended releasing her any time soon, she nervously wet the seam of her lips with her tongue and tried to smile to show she wasn't scared. Not of him or the supposed ghosts that haunted his garden.

'I'm not scared of ghosts,' she answered softly, a lock of red-gold hair drifting across her forehead.

'Not even from your past?' His warm breath fanning her cheeks, Adrian's gaze narrowed darkly. He seemed to be searching for answers, but what answers could Liadan give him that would appease the voracious hunger in his eyes?

'Perhaps I've made peace with my past? Maybe that's what we all need to try to do so that we can move on.'

'Easy for you to say. You're twenty-seven years old and your face and your body are like places on maps hardly visited by life at all. Wait until you lose someone you love and you can't bear the loss.' His voice growing huskier, he suddenly released her and stepped away.

Feeling deathly cold, Liadan hugged her arms across her chest and tried desperately to find the words— any words—to ease his pain. He looked wretched. Wretched and haunted, and she longed for him to find some peace.

'I came across the newspaper you had in your office the other day when I was in there. I saw that Petra Collins had retracted everything she said about—about your affair. So you see? You're not the bad man you like to try and pretend to be.'

Adrian's scowl was derogatory. 'Don't be fooled by appearances. I rang Petra and threatened her with a lawsuit if she didn't retract her statement.' That was what he'd been intending to do, anyway, but two minutes into the conversation he'd quickly realised that the once-vivacious actress had plenty of problems on her plate to be going on with. Adrian certainly wasn't going to add to them with threats of any kind. She'd simply decided to retract her slander all by herself, apparently.

'Why are you so determined to paint yourself in the blackest light possible?' Liadan asked in frustration.

'Did you read what else was in that report?' Looking edgy and ready to break something, Adrian jerked his head disparagingly.

'Yes.' Her voice was a mere whisper floating on the breeze, her throat all but seized with tension. 'I read that you lost the woman you loved in a terrible accident.'

'Is that what you call the murder of an innocent woman? It was no accident, goddammit!' His anger bounced off the air around him, hitting the walls of the house and echoing back to them. His lean, good-looking face was contorted with rage. 'It was a terrorist bomb planted deliberately to cause maximum damage at one of the busiest times of the day! We'd had warnings that something might go off. We'd had warnings and we ignored them. *I* ignored them.'

'You can't go on blaming yourself for what happened. You were with a news team, weren't you? They must have made up their own minds about whether it was a good idea to go ahead with your assignment, surely?'

Her quiet, reasonable voice should have soothed him. But instead all it did was press every explosive button inside him that could be pressed. Adrian saw red. 'I thought I was indestructible. A golden boy. I was riding on the crest of my so-called brilliant career and I got carried away with the idea of my complete infallibility, my invulerability towards danger. I persuaded a young woman who I loved with all my heart that it was safe to go ahead into the embassy. Only moments before it happened she was laughing… *laughing*.' He turned away from Liadan to hide the pain that shone starkly from his eyes.

'It wasn't your fault, please will you listen? How long must you go on blaming yourself? If anyone is to blame surely it's the cold-blooded killers who planted such a terrible device? Adrian…do you think that your—your Nicole would want you to spend the rest of your life so racked with pain that you can't enjoy a single moment of happiness ever again?'

Clearly wrestling with the impact of her words, Adrian turned slowly back to face her.

'Go to bed, Liadan. It's been a long, trying day and you must be tired.'

'Don't dismiss me so easily!' Now it was her turn to be angry. He was shutting her out again. Shutting her out as surely as if a wall were being deliberately constructed, brick by brick, between them. If he was left alone, soon it would be too high for her to climb and she might never be able to reach him again. The knowledge terrified her. 'You veer between treating me like some silly little schoolgirl with cotton wool for brains, or some foolish airhead who somehow drifts through life without a care in the world and without ever being touched by pain or sorrow or sadness! That's a mighty dangerous assumption from a supposedly intelligent man. Even a two-year-old feels pain, Adrian—whether it's actual, physical pain or the pain of rejection from a mother or a loved one. Without a doubt that leaves scars. So please don't write me off as though I had no right to empathise with your sorrow. I do. If I could turn back the clock and bring Nicole back for you, I would! Do you hear me? I would!' Her voice broke then, and tears, hot and relentless, momentarily blinded her.

He's still in love with a ghost, Liadan thought chillingly. And he'll never love me like I love him... Unable to stay, she turned and ran back up the path towards the house.

Adrian stood outside her room. His mind had told him to go straight to bed and forget her, but his body clearly had other ideas. Past the point of understanding any of it—his life, his work, his failure to move on in any meaningful way—all he craved right now was the temporary peace he knew he would find in Liadan's arms. Even if she hated herself for it in the morning, he knew she wouldn't deny him what he sought. He would hate himself for using her in that way if he didn't despise himself enough already.

He knocked briefly, listening for sounds of life from behind the door. He told himself if she didn't answer in the next ten seconds he would leave and go back to his room. But the door opened before he even finished the thought.

Her russet hair tumbling all around her shoulders, her blue eyes red with crying, she glanced up at him forlornly like a child who'd lost a beloved pet and didn't understand why it had had to die.

'Yes?'

Adrian didn't speak. Instead he commandingly swept her up into his arms as if she weighed less than a feather and carried her to the bed. Without words, he laid her down on the white lace counterpane, then stripped off his shirt and sweater. Kicking off his shoes, he climbed onto the bed on all fours, positioning himself above her with all the precise intention of a man who was certain that his desperate need for comfort would not be repelled—even though he no doubt deserved it to be.

Liadan's heart was thumping so hard inside her chest that she was grateful for the fact that she was lying down. Now, staring up at Adrian as his gaze burned down at her, hotly and without tenderness or mercy, she gulped and bit down hard on her lip. She drew blood and in the next instant felt his tongue against her flesh licking it clean. The eroticism of that sexy little gesture all but paralysed Liadan, and set up such a clamouring of raw, naked lust inside her that she barely knew herself. Then, his hands settling on her shoulders, his mouth moved across hers, barely touching at first, teasing her response and stoking her desire with a ruthless expertise that right then she wanted to kill him for. He had no right, she thought a little desperately, no right at all to do this to her body and her mind, to enrapture her with delights of the flesh that she was pathetically helpless to deny.

'I want all of you,' he breathed against her mouth. 'No half measures.'

'No.' Liadan twisted her face away only to feel her jaw captured by warm, firm fingers and brought round again. Her blue eyes went round as saucers as she looked dazedly up into his handsome face. 'How dare you? What makes you think I want you after the way you spoke to me? Get out!'

He silenced her with a crushing, passionate kiss that obliterated the rest of her world in one fell swoop and filled her with a fire so burning hot that she thought they would both ignite. Seconds later, he raised his head to glance down at her with sardonic amusement. 'Still want me to go?' he asked.

Silently cursing every weak, malleable bone in her body, Liadan slid her arms up around his neck and urged him recklessly down towards her again.

'God help me,' she whispered brokenly as his hands shockingly ripped the front of her antique lace night-gown straight down the middle, 'I don't want you to go.'

CHAPTER ELEVEN

'LIADAN?'

Adrian woke from the soundest sleep known to man to find the bright rays of the morning permeating the curtains like laser beams and the woman he'd made love to with such furious passion...*gone*. Combing his fingers dazedly through his thick dark hair, Adrian swung his long, muscular legs out of the bed and sat there for a few moments with his head in his hands. Her scent was all over him and he didn't feel like washing it off, not yet. Right now he simply wanted to bask in the feeling of aliveness that seemed to be flowing through his body, when every other morning he woke with the weight of dread around his shoulders and almost didn't want to face the day. It was obvious who had brought about such a miraculous change in him.

Liadan. Even her name had the power to infuse him with an excitement so great he barely knew what to do with it. His lips twitched into a smile before he realised it. Hardly able to contain his anticipation at seeing her again this morning, he reached for his trousers, buckled up his belt and wandered back down the corridor to his own suite of rooms to take a shower.

'You want me to go out with you—tonight?' Raising her astonished blue eyes to Adrian's perfectly serious dark gaze, Liadan experienced a giddy rush of blood to the head, not sure she had heard him aright.

He shrugged those wide shoulders of his and smiled

down at her with a slow, mouth-wateringly sexy smile that both angered and excited her. Liadan frowned back at him, her chest tight. She could hardly believe that he was behaving as if that scene in her bedroom had never happened. She might have responded to his urgent lovemaking with equal passion and need, but this morning her emotions felt as if they'd been scraped raw with sandpaper, while Adrian appeared completely unaffected by such turmoil. What was angering her most was that she'd risen at dawn as usual to light the fire in his study and get his breakfast ready, and left him to sleep on—not knowing where the hell she stood with anything. Right now she hardly knew whether she should go or whether she should stay and yet there he stood, supremely confident in his arrogant maleness and superiority, no doubt imagining she'd be swept off her feet with excitement at the idea he had invited her out.

Plucking the yellow duster she'd been polishing with out of her hands, he tossed it carelessly onto the piano. 'We're going to the opera, *La Bohème*, at the Royal Albert Hall. Courtesy of my editor, Lynne, who fears that I'm turning into Dracula, staying in the house too long and only walking abroad at night.'

Liadan found no humour in his statement. Inside she was wondering if she was simply going to let Adrian dictate to her in the way that Michael had loved to do— no doubt whatsoever in his mind that she might have any objections. 'What makes you think that I want to go anywhere with you, Adrian? Unless you make it a habit of inviting your housekeeper to the opera? Well, do you?'

Irked by her resistance to what he had automatically assumed would be a good idea, Adrian was deeply unsettled by Liadan's apparent frostiness. 'What's that supposed to mean?' he asked irritably.

'It means I need a little clarification here. You hired me to work for you—correct me if I'm wrong? Now we're sleeping together and obviously our relationship has changed, so I need to know where I stand. Am I your housekeeper or your girlfriend, Adrian? I can't be both.' She couldn't keep the trembling out of her voice. Her throat was threatening to close and her mouth was stripped bare of moisture, but she was determined to let him know that she was nobody's fool. If he wanted a proper relationship with her, then so be it. It might mean having to look for another job, but why should she worry about that when she would have the satisfaction of knowing she was with someone who really wanted to be with her? But right now she didn't know that for sure. All Liadan *did* know was that she wasn't prepared to be used again by any man—even one she was crazy about.

Alarm bells were ringing very loudly inside Adrian's head. *Was she considering leaving him if his answer was not to her satisfaction?* More to the point—was he in danger yet again of screwing up another woman's life with his arrogance and blithe disregard for her feelings? This was an ultimatum he hadn't expected to be confronted with, he was ashamed to admit, but at the same time he was unreasonably annoyed at Liadan for presenting him with it. Especially when his mood had been brighter and more optimistic this morning than it had for ages.

'You're right,' he acknowledged, his dark gaze wary. 'We should discuss this.'

Letting out a soft, slow breath, Liadan nodded. At least he hadn't denied the necessity for talking about their relationship—even though he was clearly reluctant. She was doing the right thing, she told herself. She owed it to herself to speak up and not be pushed around as she had been in her disastrous relationship with Michael. The situation between herself and Adrian urgently needed clarifying. It was one thing being in love with the man and unable to resist his incredibly compelling powers of seduction, but it was quite another him expecting her to continue working in his employ and still be his lover. Like it or not, this potentially disastrous situation simply could not continue. Natural common sense made her face the truth that was staring her in the face.

'So…what do you think?' she asked nervously.

Frowning, Adrian folded his arms across the midnight blue sweater that he wore with black jeans and sighed. 'What do I think?'

If someone had predicted that when Kate left he would find himself embroiled in a very *different*, less-than-professional relationship with the next woman he employed, he would have been openly scornful. He had a healthy libido, he'd have said, but he wouldn't be so foolish as to indulge it with someone who worked for him. He needed a housekeeper, that was all. And that *was* all, until Liadan showed up.

Not that she wasn't good at her job—that was half the trouble. Right now he couldn't imagine anyone else taking care of himself or his house so well. At the same time, he'd succumbed to his lust and craving for her body and made her his lover. By doing so, he'd placed both himself and her in an untenable predicament. Yet how could he not have capitulated to his desire for her? Liadan only had to walk into the same room as Adrian to make him so turned on it was practically physical torment, and right now he refused to contemplate doing without her for one second, let alone for good…

He seemed to be stalling for some reason, and Liadan's stomach turned an anxious cartwheel.

'I can't stay here working for you and continue having an—an intimate relationship. You must see that.' Her curling red-gold lashes downcast, she studied her hands intently, torn between running out of the house as fast as her legs could carry her, or throwing herself into his arms and confessing that she loved him. A course of action that would be clearly disastrous in the face of his indecision about their relationship.

'Yes, you can.'

'How?'

Glancing up, her heartbeat rapidly increased at the determination on Adrian's impossibly attractive face. The pulse in one perfectly sculpted cheek throbbed momentarily before he spoke.

'You can marry me,' he said without emotion.

'Marry you?' Liadan was glad the piano stool was situated just behind her. Her trembling limbs dictated she sat on it whether she wanted to or not. 'But you don't love me.' *You love a ghost*…she finished in her mind.

He looked astonished, as though her assertion was entirely irrelevant. His next comment drove it home.

'We have other equally powerful inducements, don't we?' A knowing smile kicked up the corners of his usually stern mouth. 'You can't deny that we're good together and your company is more pleasing to me than most women I know. You don't talk my ears off and you have a quiet way about you that I find soothing.' *Liar.* She was in his blood and what he felt for her right now was anything but soothing…more like a raging fever. Damn it all to hell! Why can't you just be honest with the woman? he demanded silently of himself. Tell her how you feel!

But how could he be honest when fear of failure was demanding he stay silent on that score? One way or another, eventually he was bound to make a mess of things. Hadn't he done so with both Nicole and Petra? Only one thing was certain. If he didn't act soon to the contrary he would possibly wreck the only chance at happiness that had come his way in a long, long time and it would be entirely his own stupid fault.

A small, disappointed shiver ran down Liadan's spine at Adrian's statement and she twisted her hands together in the lap of her jade-coloured skirt as if she didn't quite know what to do with them. 'My company is *pleasing*?' Was that all he could find to say about her? What was it about her that men couldn't commit to her as they could to other women? she reflected despondently. First Michael's judgemental rejection both of her body and her person and now this—this lukewarm litany of some of her supposedly more attractive attributes that was supposed to add up to a proposal of marriage. 'You must be desperate for a housekeeper if you're prepared to marry me in order to keep me in your employment,' she said in a detached voice, barely able to bring herself to look at him.

His hard jaw clenched, Adrian couldn't disguise his annoyance. 'What are you talking about? If I married you I would look to employ someone else as my housekeeper, naturally. You would be my companion…my *wife*.' If a possessive tone had crept in at his use of that last word, Adrian deliberately ignored it. Instead, he latched onto the realisation that it was probably the best idea he'd had in ages, under the circumstances.

Liadan was a kind, beautiful girl whose loving nature had stolen a march on him when he hadn't been looking. Plus the sexual chemistry between them was combustible. He'd got used to her being around and the thought of her not being around was—unthinkable. If they married, he would provide her with financial stability for life and neither of them would have to be alone any more. Perfect. Only, when Adrian gazed into Liadan's troubled blue eyes, it didn't seem at all as if she agreed with him.

'I appreciate the thought but...no, thanks.' Getting to her feet, she pushed away a wayward curl and picked up the discarded yellow duster from the top of the piano. 'I have to be getting on. I have plenty of work to do.' If her voice was flat, she couldn't help it. Inside Liadan was crushed. His cold proposal of marriage had done nothing for her self-esteem. In fact, right now she hated herself because she couldn't understand why the man she loved couldn't seem to return her affection on any level except a sexual one.

'Liadan?' A frown between his perfect black brows, Adrian caught her arm as she passed him, to waylay her. 'I've obviously offended you. Tell me! I want to know.'

'Offended me? Whatever gave you that idea? I mean, why on earth should I be offended by such a cold, unfeeling suggestion as to marry you and be your little ''companion''? Your editor is right, Adrian. You really *do* need to get out more. You're so caught up in your dark, depressing stories that you've forgotten how to relate to people emotionally. I may not have much money, and I may not have another job to go to if I should leave here, but at least I have a heart full of love rather than no heart at all. At least I'm not scared to express my feelings! Now, if you don't mind…' she wrenched her arm free and swept towards the door '…I have work to do.'

'Liadan!'

'What?' Turning at the door, she willed her feet to stay still even though she'd like nothing better right now than to escape to her room—lock herself in and cry her heart out. *He* might be an expert on running away from life's problems, but she wasn't. She would face whatever she had to face and afterwards she wouldn't have any cause to feel ashamed.

'I don't want you to go, so please don't talk of leaving. If my offer of marriage was less appealing than you'd like, then please forgive me. I may be a writer but I don't always necessarily choose the right words to express my feelings.'

'So you *do* have feelings, then?' Liadan was unable to bite back her sarcasm, then saw Adrian flinch, as if her words had contained a poisonous tip that had deeply wounded him. Inwardly, she cringed. She didn't want to hurt him any more than he'd been hurt already. So he might not be the most emotionally expressive man on the planet, but he still had a good heart. Liadan was convinced of that…despite what she'd said about him having no heart at all.

Clearly wrestling with those very feelings, Adrian unconsciously circled his chest with his hand as if trying to contain them. 'Come to the opera with me tonight…*please*. Let's at least enjoy a pleasant evening together and forget about everything else for a while. What do you say?'

Music was one of his greatest passions, Kate had told her that first afternoon when they'd met. And the chance to see *La Bohème* was not to be missed. Even

if Liadan was in turmoil about his less-than-loving proposal of marriage.

'All right, then. I'll come.' Her lip quivered a little
as she tucked some hair behind her ear. The decision
to go to the opera was easy. The marriage offer, on the
other hand, was far more problematic to contemplate.
Adrian didn't love her, that much was obvious, and
marrying him ultimately would only bring her down.
Just being with him would solve one great need she
had, but living with him and not having his love would
surely destroy her utterly in the end.

Recoiling from the immense wall of pain that she
emotionally slammed into, Liadan knew the decision
she had to make. Buying a little time at the opera
would be no bad thing, she told herself—because it
would probably be the last evening they ultimately
shared together in such an intimate way.

More relieved than he could say with her agreement,
Adrian felt the tension in his muscles thankfully relax.
'You won't regret it,' he promised.

Summoning up a mere ghost of a smile, Liadan nodded and said nothing.

'Here.' Adrian pushed his clean white handkerchief
into Liadan's hand, touched by her highly emotional
response to the final scene where the heroine, Mimi,
died in her lover's arms. But he was also concerned.
She'd been so quiet throughout the long drive into
London and now, in the theatre foyer, as they collected
their coats from the cloakroom her pretty tear-
moistened eyes kept avoiding his inquiring gaze; she
was clearly embarrassed by displaying such emotion in
public.

'Are you okay?'

'I'm fine.' She was lying. Especially since she looked as if she was about to burst into tears all over again.

'Liar.' Waiting until she'd finished dabbing at her eyes with his handkerchief, Adrian helped her on with her long tweed coat, her perfume stirring the air around him, immediately casting a spell he was helpless to resist. Not that the woman needed any artificial help in creating her magic. He was simply mesmerised by her.

'How could anyone not be moved by what we've just seen and heard? It's such a tragic story. Poor Mimi.' Sniffing helplessly, Liadan glanced up at Adrian, at his extraordinarily compelling features and dashing appearance in his dark grey suit, white shirt, burgundy tie and long black coat that showed off his wonderful wide shoulders to perfection. She felt like Cinderella meeting the handsome prince at the ball for the first time, knowing that these precious stolen moments together would soon be relegated to painful posterity when the clock struck midnight, and she had to finally flee back to her old life without him.

'Don't forget poor Rudolph.' For once, Adrian's smile was unguarded and warm and Liadan wanted to capture the specialness of that moment and keep it close to her heart for ever. 'Even though he should never have driven her away in the first place with his jealousy.'

'Mr Jacobsen! Who's your lady friend? How about a smile for our readers?'

They both turned at the demanding male voice and were temporarily blinded by the flash of a powerful camera. Immediately Adrian's arm swept protectively around Liadan's waist and she sensed every muscle in his body turn to iron.

'Leave us alone,' he said with a scowl, pushing past the impertinent photographer with ill-disguised resentment.

'What's your name, love? How long have you and Alexander been seeing each other?'

For a moment Liadan was surprised by the use of Adrian's writing name, then she realised that that was the name that most of the public knew him by these days. Adrian Jacobs, war correspondent, had been replaced by Alexander Jacobsen, best-selling author of dark psychological thrillers.

'Say nothing,' Adrian warned her in a low voice as he steered her deliberately towards the heavy double doors of the exit. He needn't have worried. Liadan was just as keen as he was to guard her privacy. The sooner they were in the car and on their way home, the better, as far as she was concerned.

'Did you know that you're a dead ringer for Alexander's old flame Nicole Wilson, love?'

Beside her, Adrian froze. Liadan froze right along with him. Was that why he had hired her as his housekeeper—because she looked like the girlfriend he had lost in such tragic circumstances? The idea sent shock waves hurtling through her system like water rapids. Worse still…was that why he now professed to want to marry her?

'What the hell are you talking about?'

Unable to contain his fury, Adrian turned on the hapless photographer, his hands possessively tightening around Liadan's waist as if he expected her to suddenly bolt. The photographer, a middle-aged man with sandy-coloured hair thinning on top, and wearing glasses, smirked defiantly.

'Come on, Alexander. It can't have escaped your

notice that she looks like Nicole? Still carrying a torch for the lovely Miss Wilson, are we?'

'You print those despicable lies and you'll never work again in the newspaper business…you understand?'

'Is that a threat, Mr Jacobsen?'

'No! It *isn't* a threat!' Breaking free of Adrian's hold, Liadan stepped forward, her heart pumping wildly against her ribs—not just because she was furious, but because there was suddenly a small crowd of curious onlookers gathering around them in the plush theatre foyer, gawking. However she felt about Adrian's reasons for wanting her, she still didn't want him to be hurt any more than he was already. 'Don't you think he's been through enough without you making his life even more difficult? Aren't there more newsworthy stories that you could chase about real issues that affect real people, instead of making things up purely to sell your sleazy tabloid?'

Liadan didn't know whether she'd imagined it, but the photographer seemed to go slightly red in the face, as though she'd inadvertently hit on something raw.

'Liadan.' Quietly but firmly insistent, Adrian reached for her hand and pulled her away. 'Let's go home, huh?'

'Wait a minute.' Her blue eyes focusing solely on the man in front of her with his cassette recorder and camera, she took a deep breath to try and calm her racing heartbeat. 'Don't print this nonsense…please. I'm appealing to the better nature that I'm sure you have underneath that hard-bitten façade. You don't have to trade on people's unhappiness to make a living, do you? We've just had the most wonderful evening at the opera. Please don't spoil it for us by tarnishing the experience for ever.'

'Let's go home,' Adrian said again, and this time Liadan allowed him to lead her through the thick double doors out into the street. When they glanced back, there was no sign that the photographer had made any attempt to follow them.

'Liadan?'

'I'm very tired, Adrian. We'll talk tomorrow if you want to.'

'No. This can't wait until tomorrow. There are things that need to be said.'

Pausing to rub her hand across her eyes, Liadan took her hand off the curved balustrade of the staircase, feeling so emotionally drained that she hardly knew her own name.

'Come into the study.'

There was no fire because they'd gone out for the evening, so the room was definitely on the chilly side. Glad that she hadn't yet removed her warm coat, Liadan stuck her hands into the pockets and, with a dull ache in the centre of her chest, watched Adrian stride across to the drinks cabinet and pour them both a brandy.

'Thank you.' She accepted the drink dispassionately, not even desiring it. What she did desire was beyond all possibility of happening. She knew that now.

Adrian was still trying to come to terms with the fact that, yet again, Liadan had put his needs first. There had been no reason for her to jump to his defence with that photographer under the circumstances—even though he felt the utmost admiration for her courage for doing so. He'd made love to her with unrestrained pas-

sion but had firmly and deliberately kept other, perhaps
more important, emotions under rigid control. Then, to
make matters worse, he'd made a proposal of marriage
that had sounded about as appealing as an invitation to
the North Pole for a summer holiday. Taking a suddenly urgent sip of the fine French brandy in his glass,
Adrian welcomed the raw heat that swirled into his
stomach, then, taking a deep breath, he turned to regard
the woman who stood so forlornly beside the piano.

'You don't look like Nicole. Your hair colour and
build are similar, perhaps, but that's all.'

'I think what you're trying to say is that I'm not a
substitute for her?'

Leaving her brandy untouched, Liadan carefully
placed the small glass on top of the piano. Her mouth
curved into a tight, unhappy smile, and she shrugged,
praying hard that her current feelings of despondency
and heartache would not prevent her from walking
away with her head held high. She was going to have
to be very brave and very stoic to leave this place and
the man she'd given her heart to, but leave it she must.
It might be mere coincidence that she vaguely resembled Adrian's lost love Nicole, but even so… Liadan
knew that he still loved the woman and perhaps always
would. Being second best was not something she was
willing to accept, she realised. No matter how much
she loved this man.

For a while she'd been second best to Michael's faith
until he'd finally made up his mind there was no rec-
onciling his relationship and his calling. She wouldn't
repeat the same useless heartache with Adrian. If he
didn't love her, then eventually he could only come to
despise her.

'How could I be?' she continued. 'It was Nicole you gave your heart to. I know that.'

'You accused me of not possessing a heart, remember?'

'I remember. What was she like...Nicole?'

His hands tightening around his brandy glass, Adrian frowned. For the first time in years, his stomach didn't plunge to his boots when he thought about his former girlfriend. The only part of his memory that recoiled in immediate pain was the part that recalled how she'd died. But that was a scene that was imprinted on his soul and would never disappear no matter how much he might wish it to.

'She was a fine journalist. Great sense of humour and...beautiful.' Deliberately keeping his description to the minimum, Adrian glanced at Liadan's face and realised with a little frisson of shame that he could hardly remember what Nicole looked like. Instead, his gaze devoured the pale, almost ethereal beauty of Liadan's bewitching features like a man who'd been invited to a sumptuous banquet, then told he wasn't allowed to eat.

'And she's the reason you turned your back on being a war correspondent? The reason you locked yourself away in this huge house and started to write fiction instead?'

'What happened to Nicole merely confirmed the futility and pointlessness of what I was doing. What was one more bloody death to people back at home who just accepted the inevitability of war and the casualties it wrought? People who could read about it in their newspapers over their toast and orange juice and then go to the office as if nothing had changed, because what did one more life taken in some Third World country mean to them in the grand scheme of things?'

'But it meant something to you,' Liadan said softly, registering the passionate fury in his voice.

A dark shadow seemed to pass across his eyes. 'Yes. It meant something to me.'

And in that unguarded moment Liadan knew that Adrian wasn't as totally cynical about life as she'd first believed him to be. Perhaps he was just the opposite? Maybe once upon a time he had been passionate and idealistic about people making a difference in the world. Maybe he had believed that if he brought the terrible details of war and the atrocities committed in its name to the attention of everyone else, they could share in his outrage and ultimately try and do something to stop it?

'You two must have made a hell of a team.' Her blue eyes shimmering, Liadan attempted a smile.

'We did,' Adrian agreed, his gaze distracted. 'But that was then.' Lifting his head, he levelled his gaze at Liadan, his dark eyes blazing back at her with an intensity of purpose that made her catch her breath. 'It's the present I'm more interested in right now.'

CHAPTER TWELVE

'The present?'

'I asked you to be my wife.' Putting down his brandy glass on the mantel, Adrian grimaced as though under a strain. 'Will you marry me?'

'No, Adrian. I won't marry you.' Her spine stiffening as hurt and anger swirled like a hurricane inside her, Liadan knew with the utmost certainty that she could not sacrifice her self-respect, even for the man she loved. He had all but graphically illustrated out loud that he was still in love with Nicole. He had highlighted her virtues—her accomplishment, her sense of humour, her beauty…and in stark contrast he had told Liadan that he found her presence *soothing*. Well, she was sorry, but the man she married would have to do a hell of a lot better than that to show her that he loved her. The problem was that Adrian patently didn't love her. How could he when he had clearly built a mental shrine to a dead woman?

'I won't marry you because your proposal frankly insults me!'

'Insults you?' His brow creasing in shock, Adrian looked stunned.

'Yes, *insults* me! As far as I can see, you are wallowing in your grief. As long as you carry a torch for Nicole that can't ever be extinguished, you won't ever allow yourself to be truly close to anyone else. You might play around with the idea of marrying someone because it's convenient, but not because there's an emotional connection like love! How could there be? You're so...self-indulgent and self-pitying that it doesn't even cross your mind you're inflicting pain on others. The reason you won't even entertain the idea of redemption and keep on insisting that you're a bad person is because you can use that as an excuse for your selfishness! You can't change the past, but you *can* change the future, Adrian—unless of course you're too damn scared to try.'

His eyes darkening with fury, Adrian took a step towards Liadan, thought better of it, dragged his fingers savagely through his hair, then swore out loud. 'What the hell are you talking about? You don't know the first damned thing about me!'

'I may not know a lot, but I do know that what I've said is true. You don't need a wife, Adrian, and I don't want to be some kind of second prize after Nicole.'

'Second prize?' Now he really did look furious. His mouth contorting in rage, Adrian stared at Liadan as though his gaze alone could turn her to stone. 'How the hell do you figure that out, Liadan? Nicole is dead! It's not like she just walked away and left me. How can you be jealous of a dead woman?'

Recoiling with hurt in her eyes, Liadan slipped her cold hands back into the pockets of her coat. 'How can I? That's easy when you wear her memory like some kind of invisible, impenetrable shield to prevent anyone else getting close. Think about it, Adrian. At least be honest with yourself, if not me.' She walked to the door. 'You're a man of enormous drive and talent, clearly passionate about his beliefs. In my opinion you should be sharing all those gifts with the world—not shutting yourself up here in this vast house writing the stuff of nightmares! Anyway…I know it's really none of my business.'

'That's right. It *isn't*.'

Fielding the hurt that welled up inside her chest at his acid reply, Liadan glanced quickly away. She stared down at the beautiful parquet floor with its strategically placed Persian rugs, and reminded herself just who Adrian Jacobs was and how far apart they really were. He was clearly outraged that she had expressed her unstintingly frank opinions about him so readily. But after today, what did it matter? she asked herself. What more did she have to lose when she had lost everything already?

'You don't really want to marry me, Adrian,' she said dully. 'You don't even really want a companion. As far as I can see you're quite happy here in your magnificent solitude. You were right. All you really do need is a housekeeper.'

Liadan let herself quietly out of the room, and carefully closed the door behind her. Still reeling from her passionate words about Nicole, along with her damning accusations that he was still in love with her memory, Adrian let her go without even trying to stop her. Feeling chilled to the bone, he picked up his brandy glass from the mantel and dashed it into the fireplace, letting loose a violent expletive as it shattered into crystal shards in front of him.

Even though she told herself time and time again that she'd made the right decision, Liadan had still found it hard to come home. Opening the door of the cottage she'd been so eager to hold onto, she had no sense of joy or pleasure. Instead, her chest felt tight with pain and there was a hollow sensation of dread in the pit of her stomach that made her feel as though someone had just thrown a blanket over her head and bound her hands together with rope. Her beloved home felt like a prison and she an unwilling inmate inside it.

Since meeting Adrian and falling in love with him, how could anything be the same as it was before? The morning after the row—when she'd declared her decision to leave, explaining that she felt unable to work out two weeks' notice under the circumstances—he'd merely nodded, disappeared into his study and returned with an envelope, which he'd brusquely told her contained her payment for 'services rendered'. Then he'd carried her suitcase and bags to her car, loaded them into the boot, and, with a short, impersonal wave, watched her steer the car down the drive as if he were saying goodbye to a stranger.

Now, lowering herself defeatedly into the nearest armchair, Liadan wanted to cry, but somehow the tears wouldn't come. There were some hurts that went too deep for tears and plainly this was one of them. What was going to become of him? What was going to become of *her*? Right now Liadan had no answers, only questions. Why hadn't he stopped her from leaving? Surely he felt something for her other than physical attraction after what had transpired between them? Or was the man really as heartless and impossible to reach as he pretended?

Izzy came in through the cat-flap from the kitchen and leapt up on Liadan's lap, clearly delighted to have her mistress home again. She automatically reached out her hand to stroke the whisper-soft fur, and tried to block out the memory of the face she had grown to love too well. Praying hard that whatever Adrian chose to do with his future it would make him a far happier man than now, Liadan shut her eyes and willed her aching heart to heal quickly. The thought of carrying around this dreadful pain for the rest of her life was surely too much for anyone to contemplate, no matter how stoic or determined.

'What do you mean, you want an extension on your deadline?' Lynne shrieked down the phone. 'You *never* need extensions. You either deliver well in advance or dead on time. What's going on, Adrian? Has all this horrendous business concerning you and Petra got you down? Is that what it is?'

His shoulders hunched over the telephone, his expression fearsome enough to frighten something wild, Adrian gritted his teeth and tried desperately to get to grips with the painful urge to break every piece of furniture in his study—including his damned computer! Right now he hated it. Just as he hated everything to do with his life—this house, this chair, this telephone, and most of all the gleaming grand piano that sat with such a superior air in the corner of the room and mocked him until he could barely stand it any longer. He would never play it again, he realised. Since Liadan's fingers had caressed those keys and transported him to a peace and sanctuary that he'd never have believed possible, Adrian didn't want to have anything to do with it. In fact, as soon as he got off the phone to his editor, he was going to ring a local dealer and get them to come and take it away as soon as possible.

How the hell was he supposed to work since she'd walked out on him? Turned her back on him as if the thought of him would never cross her mind again. And who could blame her? That was the thing. She had every right under the circumstances. He was hell on wheels to live with, he was bad-tempered and ungrateful, and to top it all—he'd buried himself too much in unhappy memories of his past, refusing to see the lustre of the glittering diamond that he had right under his nose... *Liadan*. Her name almost had him clutching his chest in torment at the pain of losing her.

'It's nothing to do with Petra or the press or anything like that. I just can't work at the moment. I can't think straight, never mind come up with some god-awful ending for the damned book!'

'I thought you told me you already had the ending worked out?' Lynne asked tolerantly, clearly deciding that getting anxious wasn't going to get her the desired result. The publishing house made more money out of Alexander Jacobsen's books than any other and the last thing she wanted to do was antagonise this particular golden goose.

'I did.' His expression ferocious, Adrian picked up a loose sheet of blank copy paper and screwed it up into a ball. 'But I've changed my mind about it. I need some time to work something else out.'

'Well, sure, Adrian, I can give you extra time, but just so long as you remember that your endings are your trademark. How about coming up to London to meet me for lunch? We can talk about things and it will do you good. You need to get out of that house more; you know that, don't you?'

Yeah, he knew that. The last person who had told him that had been dead right but he'd been too damn belligerent to tell her so. What the hell did he think he was doing hiding away in this gigantic carbuncle of a house that would be better off as a museum than a home? It patently *wasn't* a home. It was even less so now that Liadan had gone.

'When did you want me to come?' he asked wearily into the mouthpiece.

'Tomorrow. Come tomorrow. I'll book us a table for one o'clock. That all right with you?'

'Fine. Tomorrow, then.'

True to his word, when Adrian got off the phone to Lynne he went restlessly in search of the Yellow Pages to get the number of a local dealer and hopefully get rid of his no-longer-wanted piano.

Scanning the newspaper in the little newsagents-cum-post-office in the village, Liadan frowned, unable to believe that she hadn't been able to find anything about Adrian—let alone a picture—in any of the tabloid papers she'd diligently searched through. Could her heartfelt appeal for a little consideration have somehow sunk in with that photographer? Could he really have had an attack of conscience and let them go on their way without printing anything salacious about them? It had been a week since their outing to see *La Bohème* and…nothing. No story, no incriminating photograph of the writer Alexander Jacobsen and the woman who apparently bore a close resemblance to his dead fiancée. A week—and six days, nine hours and forty-five minutes to be exact since she'd walked out on Adrian.

Replacing the newspaper in the stand, Liadan went to the cluttered little counter, purchased some mints and a small packet of tissues, paid, then left the shop with the jangle of the doorbell sounding like the tinkling of a wind chime in her ears. Walking up the hill to meet the narrow lane where her cottage was situated, she dug her hands deep into her coat pockets and told herself she was pleased that Adrian would have one less thing to worry about since the press hadn't printed the story of their outing to the opera. He'd be able to get on with his work free from the strain of media intrusion, even if he had to fend for himself until he could get another housekeeper in place.

Unable to hold back the tears that immediately sprang to her eyes at the thought, Liadan hurried on up the hill, welcoming the extra effort required in her legs and telling herself she was doing the right thing putting Drowsy Haunt up for sale. It would be far easier to find work in London than locally and, if she found a job in one of the big chain hotels, she might even be able to cut her costs by living in.

'But you love this place, Liadan! Surely you don't really want to sell it?' Callum Willow, her tall, blond, handsome Adonis of a brother paced her diminutive front room and finally came to a restless standstill beside the fireplace. Somehow, Liadan found a smile. She'd been on her own for a fortnight now since leaving Adrian's employ and, apart from her neighbour Jack, she'd spoken to no one. Not even Mel or Jennie. Both girls were on a winter skiing break in Italy—a holiday that Liadan had been adamant she couldn't afford because she'd needed to find work instead. Jennie had urged her to come anyway—she had lost her business but she badly needed a break, she'd told Liadan. But the younger girl had declined. Her determination to hold onto her home come what may had been her prime motivation for staying put. Now, ironically, she was going to lose it anyway.

'I can't afford to keep it on any more, Cal. And I can't get work around here, either. Believe me, I've tried.' She'd briefly explained to her brother that she'd worked for a while as housekeeper to a writer, but that in the end things hadn't worked out between them. Knowing her well and guessing there was a hell of a lot more that she *wasn't* telling him, Callum had declined to press her for more details. When Liadan was ready she would tell him the full story, he was sure.

'But London? It's going to be a hell of a shock after this one-horse town.'

'I'll soon get used to it. Besides, you know what they say, a change is as good as a rest.' If she said it often enough, she might convince herself. Except that she didn't really want to go at all. Anywhere further than her little cottage was too far away from Adrian to bear thinking about... What was he doing right now? she speculated, chewing on her nails. Was he happy? Was his work going well? Did he ever think about her at all?

'You look miles away,' Callum chided, his blue eyes that were a shade darker than Liadan's growing concerned. 'What's up, Liadan? We don't have any secrets from each other, do we?'

He was right. She'd always been able to confide in her brother. Only now, she wouldn't really know where to start. After the debacle that was her relationship with Michael, how could she tell him that she'd fallen for a taciturn famous writer whose heart was given to a woman no longer on this earth?

At the unexpected sound of the knocker on the door, she almost leapt out of her seat. His eyes narrowing, Callum registered surprise. 'Expecting someone, sis? Want me to go?'

'I'm not expecting anyone, unless it's Jack next door.'

As she pulled the door wide Liadan's knees went helplessly weak at the sight of Adrian's broad shoulders dominating her doorway. He was wearing his long black coat over a black shirt and jeans, his mouth unsmiling and his gaze about as foreboding as a locked door to a shivering, hungry orphan. Her glance drank in the sight of him with a frantically beating heart.

'What are you doing here?'

'Can I come in?'

She hesitated, glancing over her shoulder into the room behind her. Following her anxious gaze and discovering to his dismay that she had company—good-looking *male* company—Adrian fought down the violent antagonism that rose immediately inside his chest and glared back at her. 'I want to talk to you and what I have to say won't wait.'

Liadan knew the dictatorial tone of that voice and resented it mightily. No matter how glad she was to see him, to know that he was alive and hadn't moved on, he had no right to just show up at her home and speak to her like that. Especially after not hearing a word from him for almost two weeks.

'I've— I've got visitors.'

'Get rid of him,' Adrian muttered through his teeth.

'I will not!'

'Who is he?'

'Liadan…aren't you going to invite your friend in?' Callum loomed up behind her, unable to hide the interest in his eyes. Desperately glancing from her brother back to Adrian, Liadan hooked her fingers into the belt buckle of her jeans and shook her head.

'Now isn't a good time. Come back later if you insist you must talk to me.'

Biting her lip, she waited for the explosion. When it

didn't come, and to her alarm she saw a secret little smile curving that rather serious mouth of his instead, she felt as light-headed as if she'd just been whisked up to the top of the Eiffel Tower.

'No, Liadan. I *can't* come back later. Like I told you, I have something to say to you that just won't wait.'

'If you've waited nearly two weeks without saying it so far, surely a little longer won't make much difference?'

How could Adrian have told her what was in his heart a fortnight ago when he'd practically convinced himself Liadan wouldn't want to set eyes on him again—never mind listen to anything he had to say?

'I don't want to say what I've come to say standing out here on your doorstep,' he said evenly, his tone resolute.

'You'd better come in, then.' Taking hold of Liadan's slender shoulders and deliberately moving her out of the way, Callum grinned. 'Want me to take a walk up the road for a little while? I'm Callum, by the way. Liadan's brother, in case you were wondering.' He stuck out his hand and he and Adrian shook hands like long-lost friends. Dumbstruck, Liadan stared at them both, unable just then to summon up one coherent word to indicate her disapproval and dismay. What was wrong with Callum for goodness' sake? Why was he acting so strangely?

'Callum, I don't want you to go anywhere. I have nothing to say to Mr Jacobs! Absolutely nothing!' When she finally did find her voice, Liadan couldn't hold back her temper. How dared he just show up on her doorstep, after the agony he'd put her through! For all she knew, there might be more of the same to come and, the way she was feeling, Liadan had a right to wonder if she could bear it.

'Fiery, isn't she?' Adrian remarked, his dark brows briefly coming together.

Reaching for his jacket, which was folded on the arm of the chair, Callum nodded in quick agreement. 'She's definitely not as demure as she looks. "Butter wouldn't melt", most people think. But that's because they don't really know my sister.' Going to the door, he ruffled Liadan's long red-gold hair as he passed. 'Be gentle with him, sweetheart, won't you?'

When the door shut ominously behind him, Liadan smoothed her hand nervously across her sky-blue sweater to finger the silver locket she wore on a chain round her neck and sighed.

'I won't pretend for one minute to understand what all that was about. You men seem to have a code all of your own.'

'Your brother knows I mean business,' Adrian said smoothly.

'Oh, he does? And by that you mean what exactly?'

'I've come here to tell you that I love you, Liadan. It took you walking out on me and telling me some very painful home truths to make me realise that I can't live without you—let alone work! And I honestly do want you to be my wife. You're not a substitute for Nicole or any other woman—I swear it! Does that clear up any confusion?'

Liadan gulped. Then she sank down on the plumped-up sofa behind her as her legs suddenly gave way beneath her.

'This must be some kind of a joke.' Her wide, puzzled blue eyes with their lustrous lashes tore at Adrian's heart. After a two-week drought from not seeing her, he'd almost forgotten just how truly beautiful she was…

'Do you think I'd joke about a thing like that? If you do, then you don't know me at all.'

'How could I possibly know you, Adrian? You put up too many walls for that.'

She was right. That was exactly what he had done…but not any more. From now on he wanted to let this woman into his heart. Wanted to let her in and keep her there for ever, because, as sure as the sun was going to rise in the morning, he was crazy about her. And he hadn't lied. He really *couldn't* live without her. It was just a shame that it had taken her walking out on him like that to make him realise it.

'I know and I'm truly sorry. You're the best thing that's ever happened to me, Liadan.'

Drawing her to her feet, he smiled smoulderingly down into her startled blue gaze, delighting in the feel of her slender body underneath his hands again, feeling himself growing more and more aroused until he almost couldn't stand it.

'But what about—what about Nicole?' Tears of happiness and confusion springing to her eyes, Liadan bit down tremulously on her lip.

His dark gaze growing even darker, Adrian stroked his hand down the side of her perfectly smooth cheek and smiled again. 'Nicole is firmly in my past, Liadan. For a long time I couldn't let the idea of her go because I blamed myself for her death. Holding onto the memory of how she died was like a punishment I was certain I deserved. It wasn't until you came along with your insistence that there was redemption for everyone that I even started to believe I might be able to forgive myself, and move on. Whether there *is* redemption, I don't know. But wherever Nicole's spirit is now, I know one thing's for certain. She wouldn't want me to hold back from telling you how much I love you. Nothing in this world is as important as that—*nothing*.'

'And you're not just trying to butter me up so that I'll come back and work as your housekeeper?' Unable to suppress her grin, Liadan leaned in towards Adrian's iron-hard chest, her whole body lighting up inside like a firework display at the sensation of being held close in his arms once again, when she hadn't even known if she'd ever see him again.

'Absolutely not.' He kissed her then and it was quite a while before he came up for air. When he finally did, Liadan's lips looked swollen and bee-stung and her lovely blue eyes were shining like twin silver lights that resembled candle-flame.

'You still haven't given me your answer. Is this waiting game some new kind of torture you've devised to torment me?'

Liadan couldn't help dimpling as she glanced up into his impossibly attractive face. 'Oh…you mean the marriage thing?'

'Liadan…' Adrian warned, a flash of impatience making him scowl.

'Okay. I'll put you out of your misery. Yes, Adrian. I'll marry you…but only if we can live somewhere a little less ostentatious than that big house of yours. I'm a very simple girl. More cottages and cream than pheasant under glass.'

'Is that so?' Grinning in unashamed delight, Adrian swept her up into his arms and strode across the room.

'Where are we going?' she asked breathlessly.

'To your bedroom, hopefully. To get re-acquainted

in the best way I know how. We've got two weeks to catch up on, remember?'

'But Callum—'

'If I'm right about your brother, he won't be back for quite a while.'

'How do you know that?'

'Call it gut instinct, but my guess is he wouldn't be one to interfere in the course of true love.'

'Really?'

'It's a gift I have.'

'I'm his only sister. He's very possessive of me, you know.'

His hands tightening round her body, Adrian's expression was perfectly serious as he glanced heatedly down into Liadan's bright blue eyes.

'So am I, sweetheart. So am I...'

EPILOGUE

LETTING the hardcover book she'd been diligently reading drop back onto the cornflower-blue silk eiderdown, Liadan stretched her arms wide before falling back against the plumped-up pillows with a sigh. With a contented little smile playing around her lips, she reflected what a lucky, *lucky* woman she was. Six months married and she was enjoying the kind of life that she'd only previously believed was to be found in fairy tales, or romantic movies at least. She had a gorgeous, insatiably sexy husband who kept her in bed more than she was out of it. She lived in one of the prettiest cottages in the village—albeit with an acre of garden and a Victorian folly that Adrian had had renovated just for her—and now she was going to have a baby, too. Her hands going automatically to the slight swell of her previously flat stomach, Liadan stroked it gently, marvelling at the astonishing changes that were taking place.

In a week's time she was going on a nationwide book tour with her famous husband, happy to be at his side and to show her love and pride in his success. He was a complex but wonderful, talented man who had successfully put some of his darkest demons behind him and had had the courage to start life anew, and she was so thankful he'd been able to do that. Happily contemplating the pretty blue and white bedroom of their large country cottage, Liadan sighed again and closed her eyes. When she heard the door open again a few moments later, her eyelids flew open and she pushed herself up immediately into a sitting position.

'I finished the book,' she announced breezily to the man who was purposefully approaching the bed with a glint in his eye that only his wife knew the meaning of.

'Oh?' The glint disappeared and warily Adrian rested his hands on his hips, his mouth in a straight, sober line. 'And what's the verdict?'

'The verdict is…' Throwing back the covers and scooting across to where he stood, Liadan threw her arms around her husband's neck and stroked her lips tantalisingly across his. Immediately sensing his inevitable response, she drew back with a cheeky, coquettish grin. 'The verdict is, my darling…that I'm going to keep you in this bed for a very long time. So long, in fact, that somebody somewhere might have to send out a rescue party.'

His hands caressing the irresistible shape of her hips and pulling her pelvis flush with his, Adrian's dark gaze smouldered. 'And what if I don't *want* to be rescued?' he asked gravel-voiced.

'Then that's okay. I'll simply take care of *all* your needs.'

'I have no problem with that.' Barely able to think about anything else but the promised delights to come, Adrian nonetheless paused when Liadan would have dragged him into bed. 'You haven't finished telling me what you thought about the book?' he reminded her.

'You changed the ending,' Liadan said softly, her lovely face unable to hide her intense admiration and love. 'You made it beautiful, Adrian. You gave your characters hope even though they were in an agonising situation. I'm so proud of you.'

'That's all right, then.' Unbuttoning his shirt with lightning fingers, he discarded it carelessly onto the floor and climbed into bed beside his wife. From now on, he would thank his lucky stars every day for bringing this beautiful, animated, loving woman into his life and giving him the possibility of a brighter future than he could ever have dared to contemplate. Whatever the years ahead had in store for them both, he would do his best never to be cynical about life again. Even if there wasn't redemption for everybody, as Liadan believed…at least there was *hope*. Because if Adrian's life could turn around on a heartbeat—as far as he was concerned—then so could everybody else's. His lovely, vivacious, warm-hearted Liadan had taught him that.

Get *Sweet Revenge* from

PENNY JORDAN

this month and save money!

SAVE 50p

on *Sweet Revenge*
by Penny Jordan

Valid only until 31st June 2005

9 904170 570503

To the consumer: This coupon can be redeemed for £0.50 off *Sweet Revenge* by Penny Jordan at any retail store in the UK. Only one coupon can be used per purchase. Not valid for Reader Service™ books.

To the retailer: Harlequin Mills & Boon will redeem this coupon for £0.50 provided only that it has been used against the purchase of *Sweet Revenge* by Penny Jordan. Harlequin Mills & Boon reserve the right to refuse payment against misused coupons. Please submit coupons to NCH, Corby, Northants NN17 1NN.

SAVE 75c

on *Sweet Revenge*
by Penny Jordan

Valid only until 31st June 2005

9 823346 050758

To the consumer: This coupon can be redeemed for €0.75 off *Sweet Revenge* by Penny Jordan at any retail store in Eire. Only one coupon can be used per purchase. Not valid for Reader Service™ books.

To the retailer: Harlequin Mills & Boon will redeem this coupon for €0.75 provided only that it has been used against the purchase of *Sweet Revenge* by Penny Jordan. Harlequin Mills & Boon reserve the right to refuse payment against misused coupons. Please submit coupons to NCH, Corby, Northants NN17 1NN.

MILLS & BOON®

Live the emotion

Modern
romance™

IN THE BANKER'S BED by Cathy Williams

When Melissa Lee works for Elliot Jay, she expects their relationship to be strictly business. He is seriously sexy, but he keeps his emotions in the deep freeze! Melissa is soon getting Elliot hot under the collar, and now he has a new agenda: getting her into his bed!

THE GREEK'S CONVENIENT WIFE by Melanie Milburne

When her brother's exploits leave Maddison Jones at the mercy of billionaire Demetrius Papasakis, the last thing she expects is a proposal. But Demetrius knows she has to agree to a marriage of convenience – and Maddison finds herself unable to resist!

THE RUTHLESS MARRIAGE BID by Elizabeth Power

Taylor's time as Jared Steele's wife was short, but not sweet. Within weeks she discovered that he had a mistress and that she was pregnant. She lost the baby *and* her marriage. Now she is stunned by Jared's return – and his claim that he wants her back!

THE ITALIAN'S SEDUCTION by Karen van der Zee

It sounded like heaven: an apartment in a small Italian town. But after a series of mishaps Charli Olson finds herself stranded – until gorgeous Massimo Castellini offers her a room in his luxurious villa. Though he's vowed never to love again, Massimo finds Charli irresistible.

Don't miss out...

On sale 1st April 2005

Available at most branches of WHSmith, Tesco, ASDA, Martins, Borders, Eason, Sainsbury's and all good paperback bookshops.

Visit www.millsandboon.co.uk

FREE!
4 Books
and a surprise gift!

We would like to take this opportunity to thank you for reading this Mills & Boon® book by offering you the chance to take FOUR more specially selected titles from the Modern Romance™ series absolutely FREE! We're also making this offer to introduce you to the benefits of the Reader Service™—

★ FREE home delivery
★ FREE gifts and competitions
★ FREE monthly Newsletter
★ Exclusive Reader Service offers
★ Books available before they're in the shops

Accepting these FREE books and gift places you under no obligation to buy, you may cancel at any time, even after receiving your free shipment. Simply complete your details below and return the entire page to the address below. You don't even need a stamp!

YES! Please send me 4 free Modern Romance books and a surprise gift. I understand that unless you hear from me, I will receive 6 superb new titles every month for just £2.75 each, postage and packing free. I am under no obligation to purchase any books and may cancel my subscription at any time. The free books and gift will be mine to keep in any case.

P5ZEF

Ms/Mrs/Miss/Mr ....Initials ....

BLOCK CAPITALS PLEASE

Surname ....

Address ....

....

....Postcode ....

Send this whole page to:
UK: FREEPOST CN81, Croydon, CR9 3WZ